Madness in the Family

William Saroyan (right, age 3) with his brother Henry

Madness in the Family

William Saroyan

Edited by Leo Hamalian

A NEW DIRECTIONS BOOK

Grateful acknowledgment is made to the editors and publishers of the following magazines in which these stories first appeared: *The Atlantic Monthly* ("Gaston," "How the Barber Finally Got Himself into a Fable," "The Inscribed Copy of the Kreutzer Sonata," "Najari Levon's Old Country Advice to the Young Americans on How to Live with a Snake," and "There Was a Young Lady of Perth"); *Harper's* ("Cowards"); *Ladies Home Journal* ("How to Choose a Wife," "The Last Word Was Love," and "Picnic Time"); *McCall's* ("Lord Chugger of Cheer"); *The New Yorker* ("The Duel," "Fire," and "A Fresno Fable"); *The Saturday Evening Post* ("Madness in the Family," "Mystic Games," "Twenty Is the Greatest Time in Any Man's Life," and "What a World, Said the Bicycle Rider").

The epigraph is taken from *Places Where I've Done Time*, copyright 1972 by William Saroyan. Reprinted by permission of Praeger Publishers.

The letter on page 143 is reproduced courtesy of James Laughlin.

Manufactured in the United States of America
New Directions Books are printed on acid-free paper.
Published simultaneously in Canada by Penguin Books Canada Ltd.
First published clothbound in 1988

Library of Congress Cataloging-in-Publication Data

Saroyan, William, 1908–1981
    Madness in the family.
    (A New Directions book)
    I. Title.
PS3537.A826M27   1988   813'.52   87–28268
ISBN 0–8112–1064–2

New Directions Books are published for James Laughlin
by New Directions Publishing Corporation
80 Eighth Avenue, New York 10011

SECOND PRINTING

Contents

Editor's Note

WILLIAM SAROYAN began his literary career as a writer of short stories. His celebrated first book, *The Daring Young Man on the Flying Trapeze*, was published in 1934, and he remained an innovative and distinguished practitioner of the form throughout his career. It came as something of a shock then, after the writer's death in 1981, to realize that Saroyan hadn't published a collection of his stories since *The Whole Voyald* in 1956, a period of twenty five years that also represents a full half of his writing life.

In this volume, we have brought together what appears to us to be the best of these later stories. As readers of *The New Yorker*, *The Atlantic Monthly*, and *Harper's*, among other magazines, are already aware, during the 1970's Saroyan went through a late phase as a short story writer in which we see him at the very peak of his powers. The stories of this period, as typified by the title piece, unfold the often bitter drama of immigrant life in an America of a harsher time, transformed by his healing vision and humor into affirmative acts of imagination. Indeed, among these stories there are some that seem certain to take their place beside the earlier classics of the genre that William Saroyan contributed to American and world literature.

Leo Hamalian

Mainly, in spite of the terrible boredom and stupidity and meanness of Fresno, my life there was full of drama and swift growth. Being in the streets from the beginning and going to all of the places of the city and seeing all the members of the human race there, I found more than enough to keep my mind and soul fully occupied.

I began to leave in 1926, when I was pretty well along in years, almost eighteen, after having had a full decade of important growth in the busy town. I was gone for good (or at any rate almost for good) by the time I was nineteen. Thereafter I went back for a visit now and then, but these visits were very brief, and their purpose was to check various places and people, and to confirm certain facts or truths.

San Francisco was the place that followed Fresno, and it was a whole new world, with a far better location, climate, culture, and humanity. But I traveled from San Francisco, too. I had to see everything, or as much of everything as I could possibly manage with the money I earned, or won at gambling, or acquired from the faithful cultivation of my skill as a writer—and from the hard work of writing.

William Saroyan
Places Where I've Done Time

Madness in the Family

Madness in the Family

GOING MAD WAS A SPECIALTY of the family. Until a man had gone mad, it was understood that he was still a boy. If he never did, he was not the equal of those who had. Only a few reached the age of thirty unseized, and, over a period of a century, only two or three members of the family went the whole distance unseized. More than a few took the trip several times, after which they were considered wise men, or perhaps even holy men, as if they had made the pilgrimage to Jerusalem, as, in a sense, they had.

With the women it was another matter, although most of them took the trip too; but with the help of the other women in the family, their journeying was fairly well concealed. Women on the trip tended to reject their children, their brothers and sisters, their parents, their parents' parents, and themselves. Their madness was justified and reasonable, which may have made its concealment a relatively simple matter. The demands on women for diplomatic behavior were so severe and so taken for granted by the men that madness was upon the women practically all of the time.

With the men the madness took several traditional forms, including a repudiation of God, or rather of Jesus and Christianity, since nothing but trouble had come of the Fa-

1

ther, the Son, the Holy Ghost, and the Church. Another common form of the madness was a total rejection of the human race, based upon ancient and contemporary evidence that the human race was criminal and contemptible. Oddly, however, this rejection stopped at the threshold of the madman himself, who, during the seizure, whether brief or prolonged, considered himself alone to be the only hope of the human race. His wife was a stranger—some crazy man's daughter. His kids were tricks played on him by shabby genetics. His brothers and sisters were simpletons, his parents sleepwalkers.

Yet another form of the madness was a conviction that all was in vain, all was corrupt, all was useless, all was hopeless.

In Bitlis my father, Manak, was considered wise and worthy because he had made the trip to madness before he was twelve, which was uncommon. During the year of his rage, he went about his life and work pretty much the same as ever, except that people avoided him, because anybody who looked him full in the face saw that he was on his way, and not receptive to small talk. But once the trip was over, there wasn't an easier man to have around. Difficult questions were put to him by the oldest men, which he answered immediately, with unmistakable appropriateness. In the most complicated disputes, he was called upon to pass judgment, and his decisions were instantly accepted by both sides.

When the tribe packed up and came to America, first to New York, and then to California, the family madness continued, but the form changed. Of course, this was to be expected, since America was another kind of place entirely. The whole family hadn't one member buried here. Everybody was on the surface of the country, flat on his feet, selling watermelons, or plowing a row of vines.

We were in Fresno, but we were nowhere, too. How could we really be in a place until death had caught up with one of us, and we had buried him and knew he was there?

This, in fact, was the form the madness took in my Uncle Vorotan, the tailor who worked for Bloom Brothers in their shop on Merced Street.

Each evening when he reached his home, he asked both his wife and his mother, "Has anybody died yet, to heal this fearful loneliness, this aimless walking about, the emptiness and disconnection?" And each evening everybody in every branch of the family was not only still alive but getting stronger and bigger.

Word got around to everybody in the family, including the kids, that Vorotan had gone mad in a new way, compelled by the New World. He wanted somebody to die, and to be buried so that he, as well as the rest of us, might know that a tradition had been established, that a culture must inevitably follow, and that, consequently, we might all be permitted to believe that we were in fact in Fresno, in California, in America, and, in all probability, would stay. Kids, who are supposed to be easy to frighten, rather cherished Vorotan during his madness, even when he looked at one of them and said, "Open your mouth, please," and after looking in, said, "All in order." But some of the older men felt uncomfortable when he looked at them and some of the women, especially those who had married into the family, cried out, "Don't look at me with those eyes. I'm in perfect health, and pregnant!" And later, such a woman might say to her husband, "I really believe he'll kill somebody, so he can go to the funeral, and end his madness, and be at peace with himself again."

If anybody took even slightly ill, everybody in the immediate family was cautioned not to let word reach Vorotan, for on several occasions he had gone to the family, to the bed of the one who was ill, and said, "Yes, I believe you will be the one to save us. Do not be afraid, do not hold back, the best Bashmanians are already in that great homeland in the sky, and the rest of us will soon follow." Whereupon the man in bed shouted, "I've got a stupid cold in the head. I'm not going anywhere, but you are, out of this house!"

Vorotan's madness went on and on, because nobody in the family died, even though there were eleven men and women in their eighties.

Early one morning, however, old Varujan, the gunsmith, was found dead in his bed, as if he were only asleep. At last, the Bashmanians had their first dead in the New World. Vorotan was overwhelmed by the good news, donated ten dollars toward the cost of the funeral, made a short talk at the graveside, and was instantly healed of his madness.

"Now, at last, we are here," he said. "We can breathe easier. Varujan, old in years but young in spirit, has saved us all, our first traditionalist in the New World. He is in Ararat, where we shall all go."

Ararat was the Armenian cemetery, which in those days had only a few graves, but is now almost as well populated as Fresno, and with more interesting people, including Vorotan himself.

1967

Fire

ONE OF THE FEW THINGS all of the Bashmanians are agreed
about is fire, which we love, as we do all things in the fire
family: the sun, all reds and yellows, California poppies and
sunflowers. No wonder the Armenians fought off the Persians
when they came with swords to demand that we join them in
fire worship. Why should we spoil a good thing by making it
official? We had official Jesus, and that was wonder enough.

When a building was on fire in Fresno and the Fire Department came roaring up in its red fire engines, we would
already be there, laughing, and rejoicing in the light, heat,
color, and music of the fire eating wood to ash.

The greatest fire I ever witnessed was a comparatively in-
significant one. The thing that made it great was that it was
my house. I had gone with my family in 1919 to Armona—
about forty miles southwest of Fresno and three miles from
Hanford—where there was good work in the fresh-fruit packing houses, and we shared a house bought for his family by
my uncle Gunyaz Bashmanian after he suffered losses in three
consecutive business enterprises. A small grocery store on O
Street in Fresno went bankrupt because of the lower prices at
the big store that suddenly opened next door. Then an orchard
of peach and apricot trees in Biola brought forth two crops so

meager that the place had to be given back to the bank. And finally this unlucky man bought a jewelry store on Mariposa Street in Fresno, next to D. Yezdan's Clothing Store. One night it was emptied of everything by robbers, who were never apprehended.

"Robbers?" Gunyaz said when he heard of the theft. "Not police?"

Gunyaz put all of his remaining money into the buying of the old house in Armona, so that he and his wife and his two sons could work in the packing houses and perhaps save money again, but his wife took ill, one of his sons broke his arm, and Gunyaz himself sprained his back so badly that even with a brace holding him together he could do no more than stand and walk. When he was almost entirely out of money, with a lot of doctor's bills to pay, Gunyaz took all of his business papers to a lawyer named Jivelikian and asked him to study them carefully. The following day the lawyer said, "I have found all of your papers in order. You paid two thousand dollars cash for the house and its furnishings. I know the house well, as the previous owner asked me to help him sell it three years ago. At best, the furnishings, the house, and the lot on which it stands are all together worth one thousand dollars. However, the fire insurance policy on the house is for six thousand dollars, and has a week to go."

Gunyaz said, "The house is old and rotten. I'm afraid it might catch fire some night when all of us are asleep."

"That is something to avoid at all costs," the lawyer said.

"I can't stand guard every night," Gunyaz said. "I have a bad back and many debts."

"My fee is one dollar," the lawyer said.

Gunyaz paid Jivelikian a silver dollar and went home. As

luck would have it, everybody was either at the packing house or at the doctor's, and Gunyaz Bashmanian was home all alone, his head full of sorrow, anger, and fire.

That night, when everybody was home from work or from the doctor's, he said to his wife, "Prepare a feast. We shall enjoy our good health and good fortune in this world, under the fig tree in the back yard."

The feast began a little after ten, by which time I was more sleepy than hungry. Nevertheless, I kept myself awake enough to have a little of everything, and then I began to long for my bed, which I shared with my brother Bakrot Bashmanian, called Buck for short. But Gunyaz said, "No, you must eat now. You are eleven years old; it is not time to go into the house."

He himself went into the house by way of the back door and came out by way of the front door. He returned slowly to the great table under the fig tree, a very solemn and thoughtful man.

Now a nice variety of flashes of light began to come from inside the house, but everybody was having such a good time eating and drinking and talking that I decided that the house was not on fire, and that the flashes of light were only rather large flickerings from three kerosene lamps there. Five minutes later, though, there was a large and crackling light coming from inside the house, and I decided that now the house was on fire, and glad to be. Still, I was better than half asleep and thought I could be dreaming, so I didn't leap to my feet and holler "Fire!"

When I began to feel hot, however, I took Gunyaz by the arm and pointed to the house.

"Wah," he said. "Our house is on fire."

My brother shouted, "I'll go call the Fire Department," and ran off as fast as he could go, barefoot.

"Hurry," Gunyaz shouted after him. "Perhaps we can save something."

Everybody ran to the empty lot next door, and then across the street, where we stood in a religious group, crossing ourselves, as we watched the house being devoured by a big, busy mouth with a ferocious appetite—after which everything fell into the house, and then the fire died. The light went out, the heat ended, the world grew philosophic.

The fire engines came. The happy firemen splattered water on the smoking half-skeleton until all that was left was a lot of wet black cinders where the house had been. A smell of bright living gave way to a smell of dark dying. I wanted to go to sleep. Even so, we were all of us up until long after midnight, and then we found places to sleep on the floors of the houses of various friends who were also in Armona for the summer work.

"How did it start?" somebody asked, and somebody else said, "From the kitchen stove, after cooking."

It was the most beautiful, the most intelligent, the most artful, the sweetest, and the most philosophic fire I ever saw. Even so, I felt especially bad about losing the bed I shared with my brother—the whole thing gone up forever in smoke.

1976

What a World,
Said the Bicycle Rider

GOING AROUND THE WORLD on a bicycle is no longer enough—
the daredevil has got to go around the moon on a Pogo stick
with one arm tied behind him if he wants to get his picture in
the paper. Maybe that's why I wasn't impressed when Amshavir Shamavoor came to my door in Paris, removed a trouser
clip from his right ankle, stepped back, his eyes on fire with
excitement, and didn't speak, waiting for me (I presume) to
get the full picture, which in fact I did get and didn't like.

This has got to be another nut from Fresno, I thought.
And while I was trying to think who it might be, he began to
speak at last.

"Dan, we went to Emerson together. Amsho? Shamavoor? A block and a half back of your house on San Benito?
The little green house by the railroad tracks? In front of the
brewery? Hell, Dan, here I am, on my way around the world
on a bicycle, and here you are a world-famous picture painter
on this high-tone street in the one and only city of Paris, hob-
nobbing with lords and dukes and high muckamucks. What
a world. Amsho?"

I was afraid I might actually know him, might have known him, one of perhaps three hundred Fresno boys I had known thirty years ago, because if I *did* know him I would have to make something of it, and this just wasn't the time for it. But no matter how hard I tried to fix him somewhere in the past, I was relieved that I couldn't. He came from Fresno all right, there was no question about that, but to me he was a total stranger. I couldn't even vaguely remember him—name, face, height, weight, voice, excitement, eyes or manners, which were the traditional high manners of the kids of immigrants in Fresno—comedy, confidence, amazement, health and a determination to be superior in any competitive activity of America. He was of my mob all right, but I didn't know him, and I was glad I didn't, because my wife had just left me.

At four in the afternoon of that magnificent August day she had announced in a kind of nervous frenzy that she had at last found true love and was going straight to him. Would I call a taxi, please? No, I would not call a taxi, but I would like to know what the hell she was talking about. Love, that's what she was talking about—in the person of Al Poufnique, a black-bearded American poet from Greenwich Village we had met at a sidewalk table at the Deux Magots a couple of weeks ago. Well, if I didn't know how to be civilized and call a taxi, she would go out into the street and hail one.

Our two boys and two girls were all over the house, about the big surprise they were going to spring on their mother, on the occasion of the twelfth anniversary of her marriage to their father—me. They had let me in on the surprise while she had been out shopping. So now she was back and she had packed an entirely ridiculous-looking little checkered suitcase, and I wanted to know one thing—what about the kids? I meant of course what about their big surprise for *her?* I knew they had bought peaches and raspberries and had made a great bowlful of something to be eaten with thick cream, because we had all had that dessert the one time we had gone to Maxim's for dinner. That's what I meant, but she said she couldn't decide just now what to do about the kids. She might just throw them all over, the way that woman did who married D. H. Lawrence. Why not? Love and love alone is the thing and don't ever forget it, Dan—in a tone of Eastern philosophic earnestness, or would that be more nearly Western, that love-and-love-alone bazaz, maybe out of old what's-his-name's popular hymn of 1910, "Ah! Sweet Mystery of Life," old Victor Herbert? And then, sure enough, she swung the great door open and flung herself out into the hall, leaving me standing there with my mouth open, thinking, Al Poufnique, Al Poufnique, who the hell is Al Poufnique?

Nelly, eleven years old, the oldest, a lot like her mother, came running to let me see her in the new dress she had put on especially for the occasion: "Mamma go shopping again?"

"Well, yes, I think you could put it that way."

"Just so she's back by six for the champagne part of the party before dinner. And yummy, wait till you see what we're having."

Then Pat, ten, then Della, nine, and finally Rufe, eight, came to the door that was still wide open, and each of them said something about the big surprise for their mother, but I didn't remember (or even really hear) any of it, because all of a sudden I remembered who Al Poufnique was.

Well, it just wouldn't do, that's all. Had three weeks in Paris driven the poor woman mad, just because she was thirty-seven and the mother of four kids, or what?

The kids were all right. I didn't have to worry about the kids. They were always fun. I wouldn't have had four, I wouldn't have had my wife have four if I hadn't always liked kids, always liked the idea of them, the whole incredible reality of them forever underfoot and smelling up the house with their fresh clean smells of intensity, struggle and truth. But now what was I supposed to do? Tell them the truth, or a decent variation of it, ask them to sit tight, and go chasing after her in a taxi to the Deux Magots? I had no idea where else to go looking for her, and it wasn't very likely that she would go there with a small suitcase, so where should I go?

"Back to the living room, everybody."

I shut the door and we all went back to the living room, but after a minute or two Nelly ran off to study the situation in the kitchen. Three days ago the cook had quit because it was too hot to be in Paris and she wanted to visit her mother in Montpellier anyway. And so all of us had got acquainted with the kitchen and how the great gas stove worked. After a moment the others ran off to be with Nelly in the kitchen, because that was where the surprise was getting worked out, and I began to think about the whole situation. I picked up the telephone book to see if Al Poufnique was in it—Poudroux, Pouey, Pougatch, but no Poufnique. Who could I call?

I was sitting on the delicate antique straight-backed chair that belonged to the fragile desk with the telephone on it, with the open book in front of me, trying to think, when all of a sudden I realized that I had fallen into a kind of trance of stupor or disbelief or something, and furthermore that I had been sitting there that way for a long time. The faraway voices of the kids in the kitchen and up and down the long hall had somewhere along the line faded away, and now I had the distinct feeling that this silence was not accidental, that it had something to do with the whole family, with the intended surprise, with their mother, with me. And then without looking up and noticing them standing together in the doorway at the end of the long room, I knew they were there and that they had been there for some time; so now how was I to meet this situation? How was I to look up and find them there, and how was I to come out of it and be alive, and say something sensible? Before I could reach a decision Pat was across the desk from me.

"What's the matter, Pop?"

I got up very quickly and saw the other three still in a group at the end of the room. "Why, nothing. Nothing at all. Why?"

Nelly, coming forward with Rufe and Della beside her: "But you've been sitting there that way for hours, Papa—it's almost half past six. Where's Mamma, for the surprise?"

There wasn't anything else to say, so I said, "A surprise is a surprise; she doesn't know there's a surprise going on, so it's almost half past six, so what?"

"Yeah, so what?" Rufe said, because in that whole household he was the one whose faith in me never faltered.

"I suggest we wait until seven. If your mother isn't home by then, I suggest we postpone the surprise until tomorrow, and we all go out to dinner and then to the circus."

This seemed to make sense to the kids, so we began to wait. The place became quiet again, as each of them picked up a book or a magazine and began to turn the pages, listening all the while for the sound of somebody working a key in the front door. Pages turned one by one, but nobody was really reading anything or really looking at pictures. Everybody was waiting, that's all, and then suddenly everybody was standing, almost as if at attention, or as if in expectation of something possibly wonderful, but also possibly terrible. I myself was standing, a little scared too, because the doorbell had been given a ring of at least fifteen seconds. Now, who could that be? Al Poufnique, to tell me, "I love Susan. I want her to be my wife." Would he be alone, or would she be with him, or what?

"Probably somebody wanting to sell something. You kids stay right here."

I went down the long hall, kind of slowly too, I must say, because I was scared. If it were actually Al Poufnique I was afraid I might not even let him say hello; I might just push him down the stairs and out of the building, and of course that wouldn't be any good at all for the kids. They would grow up believing America should push any nation that got in its way straight down the stairs and out of the building too.

I opened the door, and there stood Amshavir Shamavoor of Fresno. As he talked, I knew the kids were just a little way up the hall, out of sight, watching me, listening to him and waiting.

I heard him out, knowing he in turn was waiting for me to roar with glad laughter at the sight of him, to be a Fresno kid again, to have him meet the wife and kiddies, as he would have put it if he had put it in words at all. But I couldn't laugh; I couldn't ask him in at a time like this and try to be interested in his bike ride around the world. In the first place, I didn't know him. In the second place, I wanted to get out of there with the kids as quickly as possible, because after dinner and the circus they'd be tired and they'd go to bed, and if Susan weren't home by that time, I'd think of something intelligent to do, but the trick is to find out what it is. Sometimes the most intelligent thing is not to do anything, certainly nothing loaded with the imbecility of emotionality. And I was so annoyed with Susan that it amounted to the worst kind of emotionality. How could she even think of any other man in the whole world? How unhappy had she been all these years? How pitifully little did our kids mean to her? If she came back in the middle of the night, had I better tell her to keep moving—from Al Poufnique to Hal Fopkin, to Sal Mineo, to the elevator boy next door? I didn't know what to do, but I knew I wasn't going to entertain the forty-four-year-old lad from Fresno who was on his way around the world on a bicycle.

"Amsho," I said at last. "I'm sure you haven't got any time to lose. You've got to jump on your bike and race east to Damascus, and I know the ride is going to make you awfully famous. Thanks for dropping by, it's always good to see a face from the old hometown, and good luck, all the luck in the world, always."

In shutting the door it was actually necessary to have it reach him and move him back into the hall, and during this business he was speechless. After the door was shut I knew he stood there for some time, not believing what had happened. The kids tiptoed up, and I herded them away and up the long hall to the living room again where everybody began to speak at once, calling me names, mainly.

Nelly: "I don't believe I have ever in all my life seen anybody behave with such absolutely lousy manners, Papa."

Pat: "The poor guy was from your hometown. He expected you to bring him in and sit him down for dinner."

Della: " 'Amsho, I'm sure you haven't got any time to lose.' Oh, Papa, how *could* you? Maybe all he wanted was a glass of water or something."

Rufe: "Where's Damascus?"

"Damascus is not far from where his father was born. Not far from Assyria, but of course it's not called Assyria anymore. He's an Assyrian, a first-generation American. I know that from his name, but I never saw him before."

Pat: "He sounded like you were old pals."

Nelly (at the window): "He's standing out there looking at his bike."

"Well, do you want me to go bring him back, or what? It's up to you, but I thought you wouldn't want me to use up the surprise dinner and everything on somebody I can't even remember. I'll run down and get him if you want me to."

Nobody said I ought to go get him. They all stood at the big window looking down at him in the street, but I didn't have the heart to join them. Of course I had been rude, but so had he. I had actually thought of asking him how in the world he had found out where I was living, but it seemed to me that knowing how that had happened wouldn't have done me any good and would only have prolonged his standing in the doorway.

Nelly: "He's just waiting or thinking or something. He isn't getting on his bike or anything. He's just standing there."

Rufe: "Maybe he's crying."

Well, if he wasn't, I almost was. Nobody, under any circumstances, should ever be as rude as I had just been, to anybody, let alone to a perfectly decent bicycle rider from my own hometown.

Della: "He's putting on his trouser clip."

Nelly: "Well, aren't you going to come and watch him get on his bike and ride away?"

"No, I think I'd rather not do that."

Pat: "Seems like a nice guy."

"One of the nicest guys in the world, ordinarily."

Pat: "What do you mean, ordinarily. He's still who he always is, isn't he?"

"Yes, he is, but just now I'm not who I always am."

Rufe: "He's riding to Damascus."

They all watched him ride away, and then they turned and looked at me as if I were the most brutal and insensitive human being that ever lived.

"I'm sorry, I'm sorry, I've told you I'm sorry, what more can I say? He came at the wrong time, that's all. Now, let's go grab a taxi to the Drugstore and have hamburgers and milk shakes, and then let's grab another taxi to the circus. Let's just get the hell out of here, shall we?"

Pat: "Language, Pop!"

The Drugstore was jammed, of course, as I knew it would be, but I also knew it was their favorite place, and the hamburgers and milk shakes were almost as good as the ones they had loved in New York. We waited five or six minutes, and then there was a whole table to ourselves, a table for six, actually. When everybody was comfortable, a man with a tray who had been wandering around looking for a place at a table began to attract their attention. I wasn't watching; I was studying the latest issue of *Allo Paris* to choose between the two circuses that seemed to be open the year around. The kids weren't biting into their hamburgers or sipping their milk shakes anymore; they were just watching, so I looked away from the little magazine to see what it could possibly be.

It was Al Poufnique. Himself. Beard and all.

All right, so where was Susan?

She was nowhere about, although apparently all of the other Americans in Paris were.

He came and took the sixth place, the kids moving some of their stuff out of the way to make room for his tray, and he began to eat his hamburger and drink his glass of milk. The kids fell silent, studying his head and face.

"How are you getting along with your poetry?"

He put down his hamburger, put on his glasses, smiled and said, "Oh, hello. I'm afraid I'm a long way from writing the kind of poetry I *want* to write."

"What kind is that?"

"The best, the way you paint."

The kids watched and listened and finished their hamburgers and milk shakes.

"Thanks, but maybe you're too critical of your stuff."

"That's what my wife says, but let's face it, if poetry isn't the best, it's as good as nothing."

"How *is* your wife?"

"Just fine. A little excited about becoming a mother for the first time."

"Where is she?"

"Home, if you can call two little rooms home, and I guess you can." He giggled, and I knew they were almost broke, and pretty worried.

I brought out my wallet and fished out two 100 new-franc

notes, each of them worth a little better than twenty dollars, and I placed them beside his plate.

"If that's a loan, thanks a lot. I couldn't accept anything unless it was a loan."

"A loan, and good luck."

"Imagine running into you here. I almost never come here. I just saw some publicity people in the neighborhood about a job, and I have to go back in half an hour. That's how it happened I came in here."

"I'm glad you did. I know you and your wife are going to be crazy about the kid, because I remember how crazy my wife and I were about our first one. That's Nelly here." Nelly nodded. And then I named the other three, and they nodded, and the poet returned each nod earnestly, a man who respected kids, and would be a pretty good father, most likely.

"Biggest event of our lives so far," he said.

In the street the kids wanted to know what that was all about. Who in the world was he, and why had I given him so much money, especially since I had just a little while ago been so rude to a man from my own hometown? I tried to explain, but they weren't especially satisfied.

Well, if Susan hadn't gone to Al Poufnique—and she certainly hadn't—who had she gone to, or where had she gone? What was going on? Had they better go home instead of to the circus, or what?

"Home, or circus?"

"Circus, circus," Rufe said, but the other three, the older ones, the ones who had long ago begun to suspect a thing or two about grownups, were silent. Something was going on that didn't permit them to get excited about going to a place to watch clowns and wild animals and acrobats.

"Home," Nelly said, "and the sooner the better."

"Why?"

"I don't know, Papa, but I think home is where we had better get to as quickly as possible."

A cab slowed down. "OK, let's grab this cab."

The door opened and Susan stepped out. (Where was the small checkered suitcase?)

The kids busted out with laughter, exclamation, gladness, anger and questions, but all Susan did was stand there and look at their father—me. She began to smile, but I couldn't figure out the smile at all. Talk about the smile of Mona Lisa. This one made that smile look like the smile of a simple farm girl.

"Where do you think you're going?"

"I had an idea you'd all be here at the Drugstore if I hurried, so I did."

"What happened?"

"Tell you all about it later."

Nelly: "All about *what?*"

Susan: "Twelve crazy, impossible, miserable years together—and for *what?*"

"Four kids?"

Nelly: "Oh, fine. Talk about us as if we were cattle or something."

"What about this—this whoever the hell it was? Turned you down, did he?"

"On the contrary, I turned him down. I just left him."

"Where?"

"His place."

"What did you do that for?"

"Why should I throw over everything for something

ridiculous in a ridiculous movie, or something? I'm too old. It's too hot. What are we going back into the Drugstore for?"

"I just want to pick up a pack of cigarettes."

As luck would have it, as I had hoped, Al Poufnique was just ahead of me at the cigarette counter. Susan saw him, but he didn't see her. She looked at me, but I didn't let her know what I was thinking; just acted as if Al were somebody I didn't know. She seemed terrified that the poet might turn and see her. She flung her arms around the four kids almost as if she were some kind of animal protecting her family before a storm or something, and she moved them in the opposite direction, moving away without a word. Well, what do you know? The things a woman will do to give a man a surprise, or to hang onto something, or to try to make it better or different.

In the street she said, "All right, so I didn't see him, I didn't see anybody, I visited Myra Haley for a couple of hours, but I *could* have gone to him, I could have gone to anybody I might care to choose, but I'm too old, and it's too hot. Let's not get into a stuffy taxi; let's walk home very slowly, because when we get there I want us to have the surprise, after all. Happy anniversary, and I'm glad I scared you."

"I thought you'd gone mad, that's all."

Nelly: "I don't understand you two."

Pat: "Pop, what's going on?"

Della: "Mamma, I don't think I've ever seen you more crazy-beautiful or something. You're different all of a sudden."

We were walking toward the Arc de Triomphe when the kids suddenly stopped, and Nelly said, "Oh, look!"

I looked, and there, racing around the Arc, came Amshavir Shamavoor on his bike, moving with the wild circling traffic like a small colorful bird among a flock of geese.

Pat: "Look at him go, will you."

Della: "I'll never forget your terrible rudeness, Papa."

Rufe: "Goodbye, Amsho, goodbye."

The bicycle rider straightened out when he reached the
Champs, his head down, his legs moving steadily and powerfully. As he drew nearer I thought I had better shout out to
him, stop him, and ask him to please forgive me, please come
with us now to our house and have dinner with us, but he was
going too beautifully, everything was too right for me to spoil
it with a little corrective courtesy. And then he was gone, on
his way down the broad road toward Concorde. The kids and
their mother turned and watched him go, but again I couldn't
join them. I still couldn't even remember him. Not until he
had disappeared among the automobile traffic did they turn
away and begin to walk again.

"Who was that?"

"Some kid from Fresno who doesn't know he's forty-four
years old."

"What about him?"

"He's riding around the world on a bicycle."

"So what?"

"Precisely. He's an Assyrian. *They* won't be getting in
rockets to the moon or anything like that for some time, most
likely, if ever."

Nelly: "I don't think I've seen anything more beautiful."

Della: "Than Mamma, the way she is now?"

Nelly: "Than that nut on the bicycle."

Pat: "What's he want to ride around the world for?"

Rufe: "Will he get there, Papa? Will he get to Damascus?"

"Rufe, maybe I'd better tell you this now, right now,

because I might forget later on. You don't *have* to get there, to Damascus, or anywhere else. All you've got to do is *want* to get there. And *try*. That's enough to carry you all the way through. Can you remember that?"

"Sure, Papa. I'll remember it."

We all moved along, on our way to our surprising house in one of the most surprising cities in the world, and to the little daily surprises of our thirteenth year together, in the same boat, so to say, or on the same bicycle, racing through heavy traffic toward another place, and then another, and all the way around, and finally back where we started.

1962

Gaston

THEY WERE TO EAT PEACHES, as planned, after her nap, and now she sat across from the man who would have been a total stranger except that he was in fact her father. They had been together again (although she couldn't quite remember when they had been together before) for almost a hundred years now, or was it only since the day before yesterday? Anyhow, they were together again, and he was kind of funny. First, he had the biggest mustache she had ever seen on anybody, although to her it was not a mustache at all; it was a lot of red and brown hair under his nose and around the ends of his mouth. Second, he wore a blue-and-white striped jersey instead of a shirt and tie, and no coat. His arms were covered with the same hair, only it was a little lighter and thinner. He wore blue slacks, but no shoes and socks. He was barefoot, and so was she, of course.

He was at home. She was with him in his home in Paris, if you could call it a home. He was very old, especially for a young man—thirty-six, he had told her; and she was just six, just up from sleep on a very hot afternoon in August.

That morning, on a little walk in the neighborhood, she had seen peaches in a box outside a small store and she had stopped to look at them, so he had bought a kilo.

Now, the peaches were on a large plate on the card table at which they sat.

There were seven of them, but one of them was flawed. It *looked* as good as the others, almost the size of a tennis ball, nice red fading to light green, but where the stem had been there was now a break that went straight down into the heart of the seed.

He placed the biggest and best-looking peach on the small plate in front of the girl, and then took the flawed peach and began to remove the skin. When he had half the skin off the peach he ate that side, neither of them talking, both of them just being there, and not being excited or anything—no plans, that is.

The man held the half-eaten peach in his fingers and looked down into the cavity, into the open seed. The girl looked, too.

While they were looking, two feelers poked out from the cavity. They were attached to a kind of brown knob-head, which followed the feelers, and then two large legs took a strong grip on the edge of the cavity and hoisted some of the rest of whatever it was out of the seed, and stopped there a moment, as if to look around.

The man studied the seed dweller, and so, of course, did the girl.

The creature paused only a fraction of a second, and then continued to come out of the seed, to walk down the eaten side of the peach to wherever it was going.

The girl had never seen anything like it—a whole big thing made out of brown color, a knob-head, feelers, and a great many legs. It was very active, too. Almost businesslike, you might say. The man placed the peach back on the plate.

The creature moved off the peach onto the surface of the white plate. There it came to a thoughtful stop.

"Who is it?" the girl said.

"Gaston."

"Where does he live?"

"Well, he *used* to live in this peach seed, but now that the peach has been harvested and sold, and I have eaten half of it, it looks as if he's out of house and home."

"Aren't you going to squash him?"

"No, of course not, why should I?"

"He's a bug. He's *ugh*."

"Not at all. He's Gaston the grand boulevardier."

"Everybody hollers when a bug comes out of an apple, but you don't holler or *anything*."

"Of course not. How would we like it if somebody hollered every time we came out of our house?"

"Why *would* they?"

"Precisely. So why should we holler at Gaston?"

"He's not the same as us."

"Well, not exactly, but he's the same as a lot of other occupants of peach seeds. Now, the poor fellow hasn't got a home, and there he is with all that pure design and handsome form, and nowhere to go."

"Handsome?"

"Gaston is just about the handsomest of his kind I've ever seen."

"What's he saying?"

"Well, he's a little confused. Now, inside that house of his he had everything in order. Bed here, porch there, and so forth."

"Show me."

The man picked up the peach, leaving Gaston entirely alone on the white plate. He removed the peeling and ate the rest of the peach.

"Nobody else I know would do that," the girl said. "They'd throw it away."

"I can't imagine why. It's a perfectly good peach."

He opened the seed and placed the two sides not far from Gaston. The girl studied the open halves.

"Is *that* where he lives?"

"It's where he used to live. Gaston is out in the world and on his own now. You can see for yourself how comfortable he was in there. He had everything."

"Now what has he got?"

"Not very much, I'm afraid."

"What's he going to do?"

"What are *we* going to do?"

"Well, we're not going to squash him, that's one thing we're *not* going to do," the girl said.

"What *are* we going to do, then?"

"Put him back?"

"Oh, *that* house is finished."

"Well, he can't live in our house, can he?"

"Not happily."

"Can he live in our house *at all?*"

"Well, he could *try,* I suppose. Don't you want to eat a peach?"

"Only if it's a peach with somebody in the seed."

"Well, see if you can find a peach that has an opening at the top, because if you can, that'll be a peach in which you're likeliest to find somebody."

The girl examined each of the peaches on the big plate.

"They're all shut," she said.

"Well, eat one, then."

"No. I want the same kind that you ate, with somebody in the seed."

"Well, to tell you the truth, the peach I ate would be considered a bad peach, so of course stores don't like to sell them. I was sold that one by mistake, most likely. And so now Gaston is without a home, and we've got six perfect peaches to eat."

"I don't want a perfect peach. I want a peach with people."

"Well, I'll go out and see if I can find one."

"Where will I go?"

"You'll go with me, unless you'd rather stay. I'll only be five minutes."

"If the phone rings, what shall I say?"

"I don't think it'll ring, but if it does, say hello and see who it is."

"If it's my mother, what shall I say?"

"Tell her I've gone to get you a bad peach, and anything else you want to tell her."

"If she wants me to go back, what shall I say?"

"Say yes if you want to go back."

"Do you want me to?"

"Of course not, but the important thing is what you want, not what I want."

"Why is *that* the important thing?"

"Because I want you to be where you want to be."

"I want to be here."

"I'll be right back."

He put on socks and shoes, and a jacket, and went out.

She watched Gaston trying to find out what to do next. Gaston wandered around the plate, but everything seemed wrong and he didn't know what to do or where to go.

The telephone rang and her mother said she was sending the chauffeur to pick her up because there was a little party for somebody's daughter who was also six, and then tomorrow they would fly back to New York.

"Let me speak to your father," she said.

"He's gone to get a peach."

"One peach?"

"One with people."

"You haven't been with your father two days and already you sound like him."

"There are peaches with people in them. I know. I saw one of them come out."

"A bug?"

"Not a bug. Gaston."

"Who?"

"Gaston the grand something."

"Somebody else gets a peach with a bug in it, and throws it away, but not him. He makes up a lot of foolishness about it."

"It's not foolishness."

"All right, all right, don't get angry at me about a horrible peach bug of some kind."

"Gaston is right here, just outside his broken house, and I'm not angry at you."

"You'll have a lot of fun at the party."

"OK."

"We'll have fun flying back to New York, too."

"OK."

"Are you glad you saw your father?"

"Of course I am."

"Is he funny?"

"Yes."

"Is he crazy?"

"Yes. I mean, no. He just doesn't holler when he sees a bug crawling out of a peach seed or anything. He just looks at it carefully. But it is just a bug, isn't it, really?"

"That's all it is."

"And we'll have to squash it?"

"That's right. I can't wait to see you, darling. These two days have been like two years to me. Good-bye."

The girl watched Gaston on the plate, and she actually didn't like him. He was all ugh, as he had been in the first place. He didn't have a home anymore and he was wandering around on the white plate and he was silly and wrong and ridiculous and useless and all sorts of other things. She cried a little, but only inside, because long ago she had decided she didn't like crying because if you ever started to cry it seemed as if there was so much to cry about you almost couldn't stop, and she didn't like that at all. The open halves of the peach seed were wrong, too. They were ugly or something. They weren't clean.

The man bought a kilo of peaches but found no flawed peaches among them, so he bought another kilo at another store, and this time his luck was better, and there were two that were flawed. He hurried back to his flat and let himself in.

His daughter was in her room, in her best dress.

"My mother phoned," she said, "and she's sending the chauffeur for me because there's another birthday party."

"Another?"

"I mean, there's *always* a lot of them in New York."
"Will the chauffeur bring you back?"
"No. We're flying back to New York tomorrow."
"Oh."
"I liked being in your house."
"I liked having you here."
"Why do you live here?"
"This is my home."
"It's nice, but it's a lot different from our home."
"Yes, I suppose it is."
"It's kind of like Gaston's house."
"Where *is* Gaston?"
"I squashed him."
"Really? Why?"
"Everybody squashes bugs and worms."
"Oh. Well. I found you a peach."
"I don't want a peach anymore."
"OK."

He got her dressed, and he was packing her stuff when the chauffeur arrived. He went down the three flights of stairs with his daughter and the chauffeur, and in the street he was about to hug the girl when he decided he had better not. They shook hands instead, as if they were strangers.

He watched the huge car drive off, and then he went around the corner where he took his coffee every morning, feeling a little, he thought, like Gaston on the white plate.

1962

The Inscribed Copy
of the Kreutzer Sonata

GASPAR BASHMANIAN, who understood the enormity and
majesty of the human experience, who loved children (the
human race of tomorrow, he called them), suddenly became
engaged to a girl of seventeen who lived on a muscat vineyard
in Reedley with her father and mother, the Apkar Apkarians.
These good people threw a great party in honor of the groom-
to-be, Gaspar the gentleman, Gaspar the reader of Tolstoy,
Gaspar the twenty-seven-year-old philosopher and personal
friend of trees.

And everybody was invited.

By horse and buggy, by Ford and Chevrolet, by Dodge
and Dort, and by Moon and Kissel Kar, the relatives of both
sides began to arrive at the vineyard in Reedley, and I myself,
twelve years old, riding with Gaspar in his Overland, arrived
there too, just at dusk, at that most somber moment of the
day.

And the first thing I heard was the laughter of an unseen
girl, a laughter that made me believe everything was worth-
while. Gaspar sat behind the wheel of his open car and lis-

tened. The laughter came again, and all I knew was, I loved
her, whoever she was, but Gaspar said, "Who is that laughing?"

"Some girl at the party," I said.

"That kind of laughter is no good."

"It *sounds* good."

"It is the laughter of the animal."

We heard the laughter again, and then from around the
neat white farmhouse, where the lilac and rose trees stood together like ladies and gentlemen, came running a dark girl
dressed all in white, still laughing, herself prettier than her
laughter. Chasing the girl were three more girls of her own
age, or perhaps a little older, in dresses of green, blue, and red,
who were making the sign *shame, shame,* at her, scraping one
forefinger upon the other.

"My God," Gaspar said, and I thought he meant how
beautiful, how charming, but he went on to say, "how vulgar."

"Who is that girl in the white dress?" I asked God, or
anybody.

"I don't know," Gaspar said, "but God help the man
who marries her."

Around the house they disappeared, and out of the house
came Apkar Apkarian himself, straight to the car, straight to
my uncle Gaspar. "Come, my son, come into the house," he
said. "What took you so long?"

" 'Slowly to the wedding, slowly to the grave,' " Gaspar
said.

"The old sayings are wise sayings," Apkar said, "but there
may be sayings we have never heard and shall never hear that
may be even wiser. 'Swiftly to the wedding, swiftly away from
the killer.' "

"Swiftly away from *what* killer?" Gaspar said.

"Loneliness, my boy," Apkar said. "It is better to be in a lifelong fight with somebody one can see—one's wife, one's children—than to live in the empty peace of the killer who can never be seen. Come along, I'll have her mother bring her to you."

The parlor was a shambles of loud people drinking, singing, talking, and dancing, and after the cheers and the jeers—"Ah, why should you be so lucky, and I so unlucky?"—the girl's father took Gaspar to a far room, followed by her mother, several very old men and women, and four or five boys and girls. In the room was a very large bed, and the father said, "Everybody, sit down, please. And you, woman, go fetch your daughter and present her to Gaspar Bashmanian, her husband-to-be."

I couldn't wait to see who it was that Gaspar was going to marry, and when I saw that it was the laughing girl in the white dress, I felt "What a lucky dog you are," but at the same time I felt "Oh, no, let this one be for me."

As for Gaspar, he tried very hard to conceal his disappointment, and failed. To him, this was the animal girl, and there she stood before him, all composed, deadly serious, and just a little scared, just a little worried about how to be because he was a handsome man, perhaps the handsomest she had ever seen, and appropriately severe and demanding. Therefore, she didn't want to make any mistakes that might impel him to notice who and what she really was; but that was precisely what he was noticing—the healthy, bathed, dressed-up daughter of a vineyardist and his illiterate but very wise wife. Should she hold out her hand, small and white and for two weeks rubbed day and night with lotions, or should she bow, or should she smile, or should she just stand there like an exposed fraud and wait?

At last she put out her hand, but when Gaspar didn't go for it instantly, she drew it back, blushing, and then he put out his hand, but now she was bowing, and her hands were clasped behind her back, so that Gaspar had to reach all the way around her to meet her hand on its way back, but as it *wasn't* on its way back, he withdrew his hand, whereupon the girl straightened up from the bow, brought her hand out again, smiled, her face as red as the petal of a rose, but again Gaspar hesitated, she drew her hand back, and then, slightly pushed by two running small girls who were in her family, she began to lose her balance, reached with both arms to Gaspar for help, he embraced her, but only in order to keep her from falling, she wrapped her arms around him, their heads were almost together, Gaspar forgot his reading and kissed her on the mouth, while the little girls cried out and the little boys whistled, and Apkar said to his wife, "They will have a happy marriage and many children."

Gaspar stopped kissing the girl, but now *she* kissed *him*, and the girl's mother said to her father, "A happy marriage and many children, but perhaps not beginning this very minute. Take the young man to the men and let him get drunk, I must talk to my daughter."

At this moment a young man began to sing "Ramona" on a phonograph record.

The mother gently tugged her daughter away from Gaspar, who was taken away by the father saying, "Gaspar, my boy, I have never seen a swifter flowering of love," to which Gaspar, now off cue, replied, "Charmed, I'm sure."

"How about it?" I said. Gaspar glanced at me out of dazed eyes and very swiftly said, "You must read Tolstoy's *The Kreutzer Sonata*."

"Ramona," the phonograph-record singer sang, "I hear the murmurs in the hall."

He heard the *what* in the *where*? But it really didn't matter. We all knew what was going on. Ramona had looked at him, and that was it, he was there at last, and wanted to know of himself, "What took you so long?"

"What did the singer say?" Gaspar said.

" 'Ramona,' " I said.

"I'm sure somebody told me," Gaspar said to the girl's father, "but in the confusing events of the last few minutes, it has slipped my mind—what is your daughter's *name*?"

"Araxie. But everybody calls her Roxie. When is the wedding to be, my boy? Next Saturday?"

"What's he saying *now*—that singer?" Gaspar said to me.

" 'Ramona, Ramona.' What do you care what he's saying? What are *you* saying?"

But now we were back in the room where the party was going on. Gaspar was handed a small tumbler full of the white firewater of our people, made by Apkar himself out of his own muscat raisins, with his own still, a hundred or more gallons a year, enough for everybody, raki, unlicensed, tax-free, one hundred proof, and other proof as well, proof of being there, for instance, thick in the fight, nobody will ever see youth again, except in the faces of his own kids, "Drink, Gaspar, everybody drink to Gaspar." But a man of the opposition called back, "Why should we drink to him, cleaned and pressed? We drink to our girl, Roxie Apkarian, the dark Rose of Gultik." Was somebody being insulted already, long before the wedding?

"Be careful, please," somebody unseen on our side said. "We drink to our boy, Gaspar, also of Gultik. There are many Roses of Gultik for Gaspar to pluck, remember that, friends, and be careful."

"By turns let us drink to each other," Apkar roared. "There is plenty to drink. By turns to each, and soon enough we'll all be drunk. We are all from Gultik, in our beloved Hayastan. Everybody drink to Gaspar."

"Wrong, entirely wrong, the girl comes first. Everybody drink to Roxie."

"Are we being insulted?"

"Take it as you like, the girl comes first. Since when are rules to be broken?"

"Careful, please."

All of the men and the boys who weren't already standing got to their feet, all fists that weren't clenched became clenched, all except Gaspar's. He looked around at the men of the opposition, and then at the men on his side, and then, again off cue, said, "It is indeed an honor."

"Bet your life it is," somebody growled. "Where do you come from to take the hand of our beautiful girl, Roxie?"

"2832 Ventura Avenue," Gaspar said.

"Not far enough away. Who cares about your broken-down house at 2832 Ventura Avenue? Is that a suitable place to take our Roxie?"

The sides, with lifted glasses in one hand, fists raised slightly, began to move toward each other, and then Gaspar said, "I deem it a privilege and an honor to drink to Miss Araxie Apkarian."

Whereupon he gulped down the contents of his glass, impelling everybody else to do the same, each drinker cheering or breaking into song.

Thus, the fight, the *inevitable* fight, was postponed—but for how long? That was the question.

Somebody put needle to disk, the singer took off about Ramona again, and although the phonograph was in the corner of the room, and loud, everybody who had anything to say was heard by everybody else, and almost immediately the fight began to shape up again. One of the Roxie boys said to one of the Gaspar boys, "And just who do you think you are?"

"Trigus Trolley."

"Who?"

"You heard me."

"There's no such name."

"There is *now*."

"You're one of the Bashmanians, that's who you are."

"You asked me who I am and I told you. If you want to fight, fight, don't argue."

"The Apkarians don't fight in the parlor, the way the Bashmanians do."

"If they don't fight in the parlor, they'd better not ask for a fight in the parlor."

"Just wait until the fight starts, I'll get you."

"You'll get me the way the cat gets the dog that chases her up the tree."

"Who do you think you are to call me a cat?"

"Fight, or go back where you came from."

Roxie's mother went to the boys and said, "Don't fight,

we are all in the same burning house." Another proverb, or saying of the people of Gultik.

And then she went around among all of the men and said something to each of them, so that all we did for the next couple of hours was eat and drink and sing and dance, and then suddenly Gaspar was hit in the nose. He in turn instantly knocked down the man who had hit him, and I ran across the room to a boy who was ready and waiting, who knocked *me* down—a terrible surprise and insult.

I leaped to my feet, but already the whole fight was over. Apologies were made, admiration was expressed by each side for the other, wounds were treated, drinks were poured and handed around, broken glass was picked up, the needle was put to disk, and the singer began to sing "Ramona" again.

On our way home, zigzagging in the Overland down the empty country road—going in the wrong direction—Gaspar said, "*The Kreutzer Sonata.*"

"What about it?"

"I must read it again as soon as possible—tonight, perhaps."

"Why?"

"It is a story by Tolstoy about marriage."

"What happens in the story?"

"Everything, and all wrong," Gaspar groaned.

The wedding had been scheduled for four weeks later, another Saturday night, but the Saturday before the wedding, Gaspar took Roxie to a movie in Reedley, and then to an ice-cream parlor, and the next day he said, "My God."

"She's the most beautiful girl in the world," I said.

"Beautiful, yes," Gaspar said. "Just like in *The Kreutzer Sonata*, but beauty, *real* beauty, must come from inside, from the heart, from the mind, from the spirit."

"*Her* beauty comes from all over."

"I wish it did, but it doesn't."

"Something happened," I said. "What happened?"

"She lives on a material plane," Gaspar said. "She thinks only of material things. She wants to know what kind of a house are we going to have. How are we going to save money to get a *better* house? What kind of car? What kind of furniture? What kind of clothes? If that's the way she is *now*, how is she going to be after she becomes my wife?"

"She'll be just fine," I said. "You're one of the luckiest men in the world."

"If only *she* lived on a spiritual plane, too," Gaspar said.

"*Teach* her to live on a spiritual plane. That's your territory."

"I am trying," Gaspar said. "Two weeks ago I gave her a copy of *The Kreutzer Sonata*, inscribed from me to her."

"Did she read it?"

"She *says* she read it, but it doesn't seem to have had any effect on her at all."

"Maybe it's not the right kind of book for her."

"She asked me to buy her a wristwatch. *Asked* me."

"Buy her one."

"I must think about this. Very carefully."

The wedding was postponed three times, and then Roxie Apkarian became engaged to a dentist who had just come out to California from Boston, and Gaspar said, "There, you see. It wasn't love. She never loved me."

He got into his Overland.

"Where to?" I said, jumping in.

"I'm going out there to kill the dentist."

He went out there.

Roxie cried and ran away from a face-to-face confrontation with him and refused to come out of her room, and her father said, "Gaspar, my boy, she does not love the dentist, she loves you."

Two weeks later her engagement to the dentist was broken, the engagement to Gaspar was on again, the wedding was scheduled for a month later, and this time it took place on schedule.

The men of the opposition at the wedding party jeered, saying, "Gaspar, oh, Gaspar, how about tonight?" And Roxie's women cursed their men and said, "How about right now if Roxie feels like it? Right here in the parlor?"

"A man's world, to be sure," one of the prettier women said, "and a rather spiritual sort of world at that, too, but just let Roxie tug at the top of her silk stocking and whose world would it be then?"

As it is in this world and life, for the people of Gultik as well as most others, in almost no time at all they were the parents of four boys and three girls, it had been a rough fight all the way, Roxie herself broke the "Ramona" phonograph record. And into every fight came the inscribed copy of *The Kreutzer Sonata*, first as a guide to silly sorrow, and then as a weapon thrown by Roxie Apkarian straight at the head of the philosophical, spiritual inscriber, Gaspar Bashmanian, "May we always live on a high Tolstoyan plateau of deep socialistic truth and humanitarian beauty."

In short, don't count on being terribly spiritual unless you are also always slightly sick.

A proverb overlooked by Gultik, but seized upon eagerly by Fresno.

1975

Picnic Time

SMACK IN THE EYES, there is nothing like the sun, especially after six or seven days of bad weather, of wind, rain, fog, and low black-and-gray clouds—nothing like the sun again at last racing down the arc of the sky to the waters of the Pacific. There are many who can't take the sun going down, who feel bereft as it goes, and then is gone, whose isolation seems to become total at that moment, who sometimes can't remember who they are or what the chronological history is of what they have known.

There is nothing like the sun in the morning, either, coming up, over on the other side, and quite different actually from what it is when it goes down. It is always the sun of course, but it changes just a little every hour of the day. What it has in the morning to some people is also difficult to take, because it is so truly new and fresh and impels such wild expectations that time has demonstrated can't be fulfilled.

There isn't anything like the sun at high noon, either, when it is best of all to most people, when the expectation of early morning is back where it waits, unfulfilled, and the anguish of late afternoon or early evening has not yet come. At high noon the sun and everybody under it is midway, easy about both the past and the future.

It's all right, entirely, any way you have it, or any way you are under it, or any way you look at it, coming up and hanging directly overhead, or a little over to the side, or going down, although never is it entirely understood, loved, cherished, or put to its best use.

One day, on a picnic by the sea, a small boy had been moving about on the beach under a bright sun, with his little sister nearby tagging along, listening to him as he spoke, saying things apparently to other things, to the pebbles he was picking up and looking at, to the sand he was pushing into piles, to the water of the sea coming and going. The father and the mother lay stretched out together on a blanket nearby, maybe sleeping, maybe not, maybe just being there, maybe talking, maybe about the little girl herself, or about the boy, or about both of them, or maybe about the other things and people they were always talking about.

Suddenly the boy stopped, looked back, first at the little girl herself, and then beyond her at the man and the woman, his father and mother, his people, then threw away the rocks he was holding, threw them away as if rejecting them, as if they had tricked him, as if they were spurious and not what he had expected them to be. Then he brushed his hands together, brushing the sand from them, but as if the sand were more than sand, as if it were everything, or at any rate everything unaccountable and therefore unacceptable, unusable, meaningless, unsatisfying, worse than unsatisfying, deeply troubling, and began to walk to the little girl who knew fewer words than even he knew. He reached her, looked at her as she looked at him, brushed his hands again, brushing aside the sea and its enormity, turned and looked up at the sun, going a little blind, turning quickly away and quickly having sight restored, and then began to run with all his might to the man and the woman. When he reached them they opened their eyes and sat up, whereupon he began to sob with a sorrow that must surely have been the deepest and most terrible known to human experience.

"What is it?" the boy's mother said.

In answer, the boy cried louder than ever.

"Come," she said, and opened her arms to him, but this time—and it was the first time—he didn't run to her. Instead, he said something loud and angry that was unintelligible, totally entangled in whatever it was that he was crying about. This either hurt her a little or she thought he had cried enough, because she said, "Now, you just stop that crying, right this minute." But again the boy disobeyed her, and ran toward where he had been, crying all the way, and from there began to run up the beach.

"Look at him go, will you?" the boy's mother said to his father. "He's crying about something, and he's mad at somebody about it, too." She had expected the boy to stop and start coming back, and slowly stop crying, so that by the time he got back he would be finished with it, whatever it had been, and sober, and himself. But the boy didn't stop, he went right on running, and now he was so far away she couldn't hear him. "Well, what's the matter with him?" she said. "What's he running that way for? What's he running away from?" She waited a moment and then said, "Well, say something."

"I'm trying to think what he's running away from?" the boy's father said. "And I'm not having much luck."

"Were you that way as a small boy?"

"I can't remember, I suppose I was. Why?"

"I mean, if you were, you might know what this is all about, all of a sudden, and know what to do about it. Well, look at him, he's still going, not running any more, he got worn out; but he's *walking*. Don't you think you'd better go after him or call out to him or something?"

"I don't know. I wouldn't care to obstruct a man in a private fight."

"What private fight?"

"Oh, I guess you might call it the only fight. The fight of love, the fight of rage about love. I don't know. Something like that, I guess."

"Then you *were* that way as a boy?"

"I can't be sure, but I'm that way *now*."

"What love, what rage about what love?"

"It's not easy to talk about. For anybody. He can't talk about it at all."

"Well, you're not a boy of four who's crying and you *do* know how to say what you mean, so for heaven's sake say it. What love, what rage about what love?"

"For myself I suppose I can say it, but for him I'm afraid I'd be awfully inaccurate. The love I'm talking about is the love of a grain of sand, of one grain of sand, like this little golden one here on the tip of this finger, and the love at the same time of all of them, and of the sun up there. The love of everything, I guess. And the rage is about that same love, about the impossibility of it, or the hopelessness of it, or the enormity, or the uselessness, or the terrible speed of it, ending suddenly in night and cold. He doesn't cry like a small boy, he doesn't cry like himself, his crying has always kicked the hell out of me. He cries like the whole stupid wonderful human race from the beginning to now, and maybe to the end. Well, at least he's stopped at last, he's staying in one place."

"What's the matter with him?"

"What do you mean, what's the matter with him? Nothing's the matter with him, everything's the matter with him, the same as it is with everybody else. He's just fine. He gets overwhelmed now and then, and he doesn't know how to say what he feels or means, so he cries and runs off a little, trying to find out where to go, for God's sake. Where can you go?"

"You're almost as bad as he is."

"You asked me to tell you; I tried to tell you, but of course I didn't make it. I have an idea that most of all he is running away from love, because it's too big and too demanding. He's running away from us—from you, from me, from his sister, from himself, too. Who wants to be himself, who wants to be so little, and so captured and limited? He's a hell of a man, really, and he loves you almost as much as I do, but you're always busy getting your hair dyed or having your toenails trimmed and painted and polished, so you don't know what it's all about, and like myself he thinks you ought to suspect, at least. It's about the foolishness of it, the impossibility, and the damned unembraceable beauty and truth of it— Mama, Mama, what are we going to do about it? But you're having your bitten finger ends treated and soothed, and the remains of the nails polished, so you can't even begin to guess."

"Oh, mind your own business . . ."

"I didn't say I don't love you, so don't get defensive, too. Having you innocent and totally unaware is enough for him to

fight about, and for me, too. I wouldn't be able to begin to tell
you how much I love you, even for the business with the hair
and the toenails and the fingernails, and the self-consciousness
about the ears and the nostrils, and the lower lip that you think
is too thick or something. Nostrils are nostrils. They are perfectly all right. Yours happen to be perfect. When I kiss you,
like this, you mustn't imagine my idea is to inspect them."

"If you love me so much why do you find so much fault
with me?"

"I'm a fault-finder. It isn't actually that you're stupid,
it's just that you don't give yourself half a chance. You're
actually brighter than anybody in this damned family, although I think the boy is going to be brighter, and the girl is
going to use her brightness better. Well, he's on his way back."

"Do you think he's crying?"

"I think he isn't."

"Well, what was it exactly that happened?"

"He felt the enormity of being here, of being alive, under
the sun, a part of love, of the love that is in everything, and he
wanted to do something about it, something as big as the love
itself—you and I kiss and hold one another and beg and begat,
and let the rest of the bigness go, but he can't do that, and it
infuriates him. What he would really like to do, most likely,
is to ravage the whole thing. Well, it can't be done, can it,
by anybody, let alone by a four-year-old boy."

"Why in the world would he want to ravage it?"

"So he would have had it before it's gone, that's why.
Before *he* is gone, you understand, although to him it all
started when he did and it will all stop when he does—until
he's ten or eleven, I guess, and starts getting it straight, or
maybe crooked. Now, when he gets here for God's sake don't

bring up the matter, will you? He's finding out, he's doing all right, he'll go to school but nobody's going to teach him anything. It's all in him from the beginning waiting to come out, waiting for some accident like this one to bring it out."

"What accident?"

"I think this all started when he suddenly noticed the sun for the first time. It was an accident that he began to notice it, an inevitable accident and one of the best, but still an accident. A lot of unlucky people take years to have that accident, and a lot never have it."

"What is it about the sun, and you, and him? Do you think it's yours and nobody else's, or what? It's not your private property, it's everybody's, although a lot of us aren't crazy about it. I happen to prefer night and the moon and the stars."

"They're very nice, too. Here he is, then, and leave him alone."

The boy came and stood in front of both of them, not smiling, dry-eyed, sober, and in a soft voice he asked: "When do we do the picnic part?"

"How about right now?" the boy's mother said, and his father reached back and took the picnic basket by the handle and set it down at the center of the blanket.

"Picnic time," the boy shouted to his sister, and the little girl got up and began to walk, not run, toward the rest of the family.

1973

A Fresno Fable

KEROPE ANTOYAN, the grocer, ran into Aram Bashmanian, the lawyer, in the street one day and said, "Aram, you are the very man I have been looking for. It is a miracle that I find you this way at this time, because there is only one man in this world I want to talk to, and you are that man, Aram."

"Very well, Kerope," the lawyer said. "Here I am."

"This morning," the grocer said, "when I got up I said to myself, 'If there is anybody in this whole world I can trust, it is Aram,' and here you are before my eyes—my salvation, the restorer of peace to my soul. If I had hoped to see an angel in the street, I would not have been half so pleased as I am to see you, Aram."

"Well, of course I can always be found in my office," Aram said, "but I'm glad we have met in the street. What is it, Kerope?"

"Aram, we are from Biltis. We understand all too well that before one speaks one thinks. Before the cat tastes the fish, his whiskers must feel the head. A prudent man does not open an umbrella for one drop of rain. Caution with strangers, care with friends, trust in one's very own—as you are my very own, Aram. I thank God for bringing you to me at this moment of crisis."

53

"What is it, Kerope?"

"Aram, every eye has a brow, every lip a mustache, the foot wants its shoe, the hand its glove, what is a tailor without his needle, even a lost dog remembers having had a bone, until a candle is lighted a prayer for a friend cannot be said, one man's ruin is another man's reward."

"Yes, of course, but what is the crisis, Kerope?"

"A good song in the mouth of a bad singer is more painful to the ear than a small man's sneeze," the grocer said.

"Kerope," the lawyer said. "How can I help you?"

"You are like a brother to me, Aram—a younger brother whose wisdom is far greater than my own, far greater than any man's."

"Well, thank you, Kerope," Aram said, "but *please* tell me what's the matter, so I can try to help you."

In the end, though, Kerope refused to tell Aram his problem.

Moral: If you're really smart, you won't trust even an angel.

1976

Lord Chugger of Cheer

THE BICYCLE IS A CITY THING, virtually useless anywhere excepting on a pavement or hard surface of some kind. Without the road it would never have been invented. It is a little mad, both in design and purpose. Two wheels held together in a frame, with a simple mechanical system enabling a forward movement for one person.

As a small boy, whenever I saw a man on a bicycle, I considered him part of it, an eccentricity, another order of human creature, perhaps some kind of angel. The little ringing bells on the handlebars heightened this misconception.

I longed for the time when I would have a bicycle of my own and be a bicycle rider.

One day my son said, "Buy me a bicycle." He was five years old, standing at the living room window, looking down at the street. "Like that."

I went to the window, and across the street I saw a Western Union boy getting on his bike after delivering a telegram, and then I saw him take off and go.

Well, I just couldn't be disrespectful of anything that might be involved here, which was in fact at least a little mystical, as if my son were myself asking somebody, had there been somebody to ask, to get me what I wanted when I wanted it. I felt that somebody somewhere sometime ought to be permitted to have his wish granted, and so I took him down to the street.

We got into my car and drove to a place I knew near the Kezar Stadium where bicycles were certainly rented to people, especially on Sundays, and where they were surely also sold. I couldn't quite believe they would have a bicycle for a boy so small, but I wasn't sure, and in any case I wanted him to go into a place like that, full of all kinds of bicycles, to see the man there, to have the man see *him*, to hear him talk, to watch him bring out the nearest thing he had to something that might be appropriate.

"Are we going somewhere to get my bicycle?" he said.

"We're going to a bicycle shop to see if the man has one for you."

"He *has*."

"We'll see it, then, and if you like it, you can have it."

He was hushed with astonishment, excitement, and possibly even a little fear. Our luck was good: There was a parking place directly in front of the store. We went in, as if into heaven itself. The man in the shop was sixty or so, mid-European, possibly Czech, of medium height, heavy in the shoulders, thick brown hair, black smears on hands and face, a man I knew my son considered one of the great ones of the world.

"Have you a bicycle this boy might learn to ride?"

"This *big* boy?" the man said. The word impelled levitation in my son. He literally left the floor at the sound of it, apparently helplessly dancing. "I've got a bicycle back there, maybe just right, red, brand-new, but sixty-five dollars."

"I'll take it."

"But you haven't seen it yet."

. . .

He went to the back of the shop, out of sight, and began to move bikes around, so that he could get to the one that was red.

My son nodded in reply, and I knew why. He was speechless. He was *breathing* all right, but somewhere along the line he *had* stopped breathing and then had started again, but he wasn't quite ready yet to start talking again.

After two minutes of anxious waiting, my son saw the man appear in the narrow aisle between bicycles, holding the handlebars of the smallest bicycle I had ever seen, and strong, beautifully designed, not merely something from a factory but something from where they have everything—for everybody.

"Do you like it?" the man said to the boy, and then to me, "What's his name?"

"Chugger."

"Do you like it, Chugger?"

My son nodded to the man and then looked at me, as if to ask, "Do you?" I brought out my wallet and counted out seventy dollars.

"Put him on the saddle," the man said. "Let him get his feet on the pedals, his hands on the handlebars, so if it's not just right, I can *make* it just right."

This was done, and the man moved off a little to stand and study the situation.

"Feel all right?" he said to my son.

My son nodded.

"I'll *tighten* everything, then."

My son watched him work with the small tools, and then the man took the money, made a bill of sale, gave me five dollars in change, a brown envelope containing an illustrated booklet describing the bike, a guarantee certificate, and two small tools.

I thanked the man, my son nodded good-bye to him, and I got the bike into the back part of the car, on the plush upholstery. We drove home, and I took the bike up to the flat. His little sister couldn't believe her eyes, and his mother thought I was mad.

"Out of the house with it, down to the cement terrace in the backyard. There's plenty of room down there to have him fall and break his leg."

He didn't fall, didn't break his leg, but *did* almost learn to ride, in well under an hour. He was so pleased and proud he permitted his sister to sit on the seat and be wheeled around, as if she were learning, too.

The next day he learned to ride well enough to fall safely whenever he lost his balance, but he insisted on getting right back on and trying again—alone. I could watch, but that was all. Who said he couldn't ride a bike? Who said he was too small?

The third day he rode quite well, knew how to keep the thing under control, and how to keep his balance.

"Where can I go?" he said.

I was sure he meant out to the sidewalk, to the street, where he had seen the telegraph messenger, but I thought I'd better let *him* tell me where he wanted to go.

"Where?" I said.

"Where the bicycle riders go."

"Where the bicycle riders *go?*"

"They go somewhere, don't they?"

"They *do*, of course."

"Where?"

"Wherever they want to go."

"Far away?"

"Sometimes, but it's always, home again, afterward. Where would you *like* to go?"

"Far away."

"Really?"

"Farther away than any other bicycle rider."

"Why?"

"I want to *be* there."

"Why?" I said.

He looked at me as if I had asked the rudest question anybody could possibly ask anybody else.

"*Why?* Didn't you go there?"

"Well, yes, I did. I believe I did."

"Well, I want to go, too," he said.

And then, in a voice so hushed it could barely be heard: "Where is it?"

"Everywhere, actually," I said. And as luck would have it—good luck, that is, good luck for me, that is—his mother came out onto the back porch and said, "Okay now, up for lunch, and then your nap."

"Five minutes?" he said.

"No, *now*," his mother said. "You've got to wash, and everything's on the table."

After his nap, again by good luck, I was in town, so he

rode his bike on the terrace in the backyard. When I got home, it was night, and there were new things in the world now. After his bath and supper, he came with his sister for the talk before bed, or the telling or reading of stories, the told ones more esteemed than the read ones because the told ones were about the teller himself long ago, and suddenly he said, "When did you get your first bike?"

"I *shared* my brother's bike when I was nine."

"Nine? That old?"

"But I didn't get my own bike until I was twelve."

"Why didn't you? Didn't you *want* your own bike?"

"I wanted it, but . . . let me see how I can put this."

"Put it the way it was," his mother said. "You didn't have any money."

"Okay, but that wasn't the only reason."

"What was the other reason?" he said.

"He wanted a pair of shoes first," his mother said.

"That's true, too."

"And *nobody* gets anything just because he wants it," she said.

"*I* do," the boy said. "I got my bike, didn't I?"

"Yes, you did," his mother said, "and all I can say is, have you got a lot to learn! The other reason he didn't get his bike before he was twelve was that his father didn't buy it for him."

"Why didn't he?"

"His father was dead."

"Why didn't your mother buy it for you?"

"His mother was poor."

"Your other people, why didn't *they* buy it for you?"

"His other people were poor, too, and couldn't buy bicycles for *themselves.*"

"That's what you think," I said. "My father *wasn't* dead, he'd gone away to gather material for a new book. My mother wasn't poor, she had more of everything worth having than anybody else in the world. My other people weren't poor, either—it was just that in our family it was considered bad manners for anybody to accept gifts from anybody excepting his own father or his own mother. All of my other people wanted to buy me a bicycle, but I wouldn't let them, Lady Loudmouth."

"Lady Loudmouth," my daughter said. "That's a very funny name. Call me a funny name, too, Papa."

"Lady Lovelight."

"Off to bed, then, the both of you," their mother said.

"A funny name for me, too, first," the boy said.

"Chugger. You've had the name almost all your life. You were born on a bicycle, chugging for all you were worth, on your way to that faraway place everybody wants to reach but few do."

"What place?" my son said.

"Here. Right here. Right now. Remember that. Remember it always, Lord Chugger."

"Lord Chugger?"

"Lord Chugger of Cheer."

"Yaaaaay," he said, as his mother dragged him off. "Lord Chugger of Cheer, that's who I am, and you know where Cheer is."

He took some bad falls on the little red bike, got up

from them in raging tears, furious with himself, with the bike, with his father, with his mother, with the world, and the whole mystical fantasy and truth of it, but he was always soon back with them all, and home again—more and more with them every day, but also every day less. And less.

1971

Cowards

COWARDS ARE THE NICEST PEOPLE, the most interesting, the gentlest, the most refined, the least likely to commit crimes. They wouldn't think of robbing a bank. They have no wish to assassinate a President. If a ditchdigger calls him a bastard for accidentally kicking dirt into his eyes, a coward doesn't feel his honor has been sullied and he must therefore fight the ditchdigger and take an awful beating. He says, "I'm sorry, I really didn't mean to do that," and goes about his business.

Cowards are decent. They are thoughtful.

When the Selective Service Act reached into Armenian Town in Fresno in 1917, the eligible sons of the various families making their homes there presented themselves to the draft board in the hall of Emerson School and were soon in training camp at Camp Curry in Yosemite National Park. The government wanted them, who were they to argue with the government?

At this time, however, a man of twenty-four named Kristofor Agbadashian, who lived with his mother and three unmarried sisters in the house at number 123 M Street, who for three years had been employed at Cooper's Department Store in the menswear department, disappeared.

Suddenly it was noticed that he did not leave his house

precisely at 8:15 every morning and walk to work, easily the best-dressed man in the whole neighborhood, right down to the pearl stickpin in his tie and the red rosebud in his lapel. Well, of course, a lot of young men in the neighborhood had been drafted and had disappeared, so there was no reason for anybody to wonder about the actual whereabouts of Kristofor. Inquiries about him at Cooper's were answered by the remark that he was away, which, of course, was true.

As for his mother, whenever one of the mothers of the neighborhood who had had one or two sons drafted discreetly, cautiously, and even sympathetically asked about the whereabouts and well-being of Kristofor, saying perhaps, "Ahkh, my dear Aylizabet, I miss seeing handsome Kristofor on his way to work every morning, has the poor boy been drawn into the war by the government, as my Simon and Vask have been?" Kristofor's mother said, "Yes, Kristofor has been taken also. God protect him, and your sons as well."

And of course there was no reason for anybody to disbelieve this reply, or to look into the matter further. However, when official-looking Fords and Chevrolets stopped in front of the neat white little house at 123 M Street, and important-looking Americans stepped out of these automobiles and went up to the front door, and then on into the house, everybody in the neighborhood began to wonder what was going on. Was it possible that Kristofor had already lost his life, and the important-looking Americans, surely employed by the government, were calling on the boy's mother and sisters to break the word gently, and to pay homage to Kristofor for being the first in Armenian Town to give his life for the government? But when a month later three cars stopped in front of the house and more important-looking people than ever stepped out of the cars, including a man wearing a sheriff's badge and a revolver in holster, the people of the neighborhood began to suspect that something might be not quite right.

Packing figs at Guggenheim's, the mother Aylizabet one day said to her best friend, Arshaluce Ganjakian, "Please try to understand my nervousness. I can't sleep, I can't rest, for anxiety about my son. We believed he had been taken into the Army, the same as all of our other boys, but they tell us no, he isn't in the Army, so then, my dear Arshaluce, where is he? It would be a thousand times better if he were in the Army, and sent me a letter once a month. Six months now, and not one word. I can only pray that nothing terrible has happened to him."

"Ah, he's a good boy," the friend said. "God will look after him, although I hope he hasn't gone somewhere and lost himself in a life of sin. In a big city like San Francisco perhaps, or Chicago, or even New York. I will light a candle for him at church this Sunday and say a prayer, for he is a good boy." And then, after working swiftly in silence for half an hour or more, to earn perhaps as much as two dollars for a ten-hour day, the friend said, "Or, what's worse even than a life of sin somewhere, I pray to God he hasn't gone to a river and drowned himself, as other young men have done, because they do not believe in war and refuse to be soldiers. Only night before last my youngest, Yedvard, read about such a boy in *The Evening Herald*."

"Drowned himself?" Aylizabet said.

"In Kings River," the friend said. "Wrote his note, took off his clothes, and drowned himself."

"Poor boy, whoever he was."

"A German boy. There are many of them in Kingsburg."

"Poor dear German boy, how can the government ask him to kill his own brothers?"

"Nobody can help *him*," the friend said. "He's gone. The police suspected a trick, dragged the river, found his body, and so his people buried him, but nobody went to the funeral except his own father and mother and brothers and sisters. It was all in the paper, which said friends of the family were afraid to go to the funeral, since they are all Germans."

"The poor father, the poor mother, the poor little brothers and sisters," Aylizabet said. "I love them all, whoever they are."

"Germans," Arshaluce said. "Enemies. All of a sudden they are enemies, but after the war will they still be enemies? The boy will still be drowned. Even a life of sin in a big city is better than to be drowned, because after the war the sinner will still be alive, at any rate. There is always such a thing as redemption. He can start all over again. He can speak to the Holy Father at the Holy Church and be born again. He can take a nice Armenian girl for his wife and start a family of his own. A life of sin, any life at all, is better than to be drowned, because the war will end, every war ends, and he will still be only a young man. I will light a candle and say a prayer for Kristofor. Do not be nervous about your son, Aylizabet, there is a God in Heaven."

And so the new word in the neighborhood about Kristofor was, "He is gone, he has disappeared, he has written his mother no letter in six months, he may be living a life of sin in San Francisco, or he may have drowned himself, remember him in your prayers."

And there the matter stood for many months.

Haigus Baboyan mailed postcards from Paris of the Eiffel Tower, the Arc de Triomphe, and the Tuileries to the nine members of the Sunday School class he had taught at the First Armenian Presbyterian Church, saying uplifting things like, "The streets of Paris are full of men born crippled because of syphilis in their fathers." And so on.

Gissag Jamanakian was killed at Verdun, Vaharam Vaharamian at Chateau-Thierry, and the Kasabian twins, Krikor and Karekin, at Belleau Wood. All under twenty-five years of age, all brought to Fresno from Armenia when they were still babes in arms or small boys. But there were many others, too—killed in action in France, in Flanders Field, in Normandy, or somewhere else. A number of unlucky fellows died at Camp Curry of influenza, almost as if they hadn't been in the war at all. Two or three went over the hill from that camp to San Francisco, but after a week or two returned, were given medical examinations, and then were only mildly punished. A half-dozen boys of the neighborhood were gassed, but survived. And Hovsep Lucinian, hit by shrapnel and left for dead in an area under bombardment called no-man's-land, made his peace with himself and considered himself as good as dead when somebody came crawling and dragged him to safety. This turned out to be the one man in his company Hovsep hadn't liked, had in fact considered an enemy—an Assyrian boy from

Turlock named Joe Assouri. They became friends for life, although they had frequent fallings-out, whereupon Joe would shout, "I was a damned fool to risk my life to save yours." And Hovsep would shout back, "I am only waiting for the day when I shall be able to save your life. After that, forget it." These outbursts were at poker games, when both men had large families of kids by American girls. Kids who spoke neither Armenian nor Assyrian but kept their names and looked for all the world precisely as they should—altogether Assyrian and Armenian, but with just a little something unaccountable added.

In Guggenheim's, early in October of 1918, Kristofor's mother Aylizabet said to her best friend, Arshaluce Ganjakian, "Is it true that the war will soon end?"

"Yes," Arshaluce said, "Yedvard reads about it in *The Evening Herald* every night. Soon now our boys will all come home. I shall see my Mihran soon, and you will see your Kristofor, I'm sure, wherever he is. Have you still had no word?"

"None," Aylizabet said. "Almost two full years, not one word."

But for longer than a year the whole neighborhood had had word about Kristofor, which they both believed and disbelieved. It came about because of something said by Ash Bashmanian, who, after selling papers every evening, went to the Liberty Theater because admission for him was only a copy of the paper handed to the ticket-taker, and did not leave until after the last show, which for Fresno was rather late, a little before midnight. When Ash got home and sat down to his supper he told his father, "I saw Kristofor tonight."

After a few minutes his father said, "I wasn't listening.

I'm worried about you at the movies every night. What did you say?"

"Kristofor," Ash said. "I saw him."

"Kristofor Agbadashian?"

"Yes. The Cooper's menswear man."

"You imagined it," the father said. "From seeing so many movies."

"No, I saw him."

"He's been gone almost two whole years. How could you see him?"

"He came back, I guess," Ash said.

"From where?" the father said. "Was he in uniform?"

"No, he was wearing the same clothes he always wears."

"Where'd he go?"

"Home."

"What home?"

"On M Street. I saw him go into his house, and I came on home."

"Keep this to yourself, please," the father said.

"Why?"

"Just keep it to yourself. You can't see straight from seeing movies, and Kristofor is wanted by the government. Let's forget all about it. You didn't see anything. I'll give you a dollar."

"I don't want a dollar," Ash said. "I sell papers every day to bring home money, to help out. I won't tell anybody, but I *did* see him."

Somebody else must have seen him, too, because it was soon all over the neighborhood that Kristofor Agbadashian was home. He had either run away and come back, or he had been hiding in the house at 123 M Street all the time, until finally it had become too much for him and he had taken to going out to walk late at night.

"Where's he been?" the joke went.

"Under the bed," came the answer.

And so, of course, the word of the neighborhood had reached Kristofor's mother's best friend, Arshaluce Ganjakian, if, in fact, it had not also reached Kristofor's mother herself.

A few days after their talk about the probability that the war would soon end, Aylizabet Agbadashian said to Arshaluce Ganjakian, "Arshaluce, my dear friend, I must tell you something on our way home from work tonight, or I'm afraid I shall die." On their way home, when she was sure no one else would overhear them, she said, "Kristofor did not go anywhere. He has been home all this time. It is my fault. I told him I would die if he went away. His father died when he was still a small boy. I could not bear to lose the only man remaining in my family. But now what shall I do? What will happen to him when the war ends and everybody comes home? It is all my fault, not his, I swear it. Help me. I know I can trust you not to tell anybody, but please help me, and someday I will help you. What shall I do? What shall we do?"

On November 11, 1918, the war ended. And that was that, except for the drowned boy in Kingsburg, the dead of the neighborhood in France, the dead from influenza at Camp Curry, and the disgraced Kristofor Under the Bed, as he came to be called by everybody. But nobody looked down at him, and nobody looked down at his mother. Only Kristofor and his mother knew what they had done and why they had done it. Nobody else could even guess. Whatever it had been, *however* it had been, it was something between themselves and God alone, not the government, which of course had much, much more between itself and God alone.

For weeks and months, as the boys of the neighborhood came home and got back into their proper clothes, there was happy confusion in Armenian Town, with only an occasional outbreak of sorrow, and almost always on the part of the strongest men, such as Shulavary Bashmanian, who, when he was asked for whom he was crying, since he had had no son in the war, said, "For Kristofor. Crucified for his bravery. Coward he was, no doubt, but how much more brave a man must be to be a coward. It is easy to be a soldier of the government with all of your comrades. But it is very hard to be yourself, all alone under the bed in your mother's house. I am crying for the bravery of Kristofor. The war is over. Whoever won, won *without* Kristofor. May God forgive the winners and the loser alike, they each have their dead. May God protect Kristofor Under the Bed, wherever he may be or wherever he may go."

As a matter of fact, several weeks before the signing of the Armistice, he went to Sacramento and under the name of Charles Abbott took a job in the menswear department of Roos Bros., who soon invited him to take a better job at more money at the store in San Francisco, where he stayed for three years, at which time he opened his own store on Post Street.

It was there six years later that the government caught up with him. He was married to a Scotch-Irish girl from Boston, a graduate of Smith, and they had had three sons and a daughter. Two of his sisters had married, one had died, and his mother lived alone in the house at 123 M Street, now and then visited by her daughters and their husbands and kids.

The man from the government, who was in his late six-ties, by name Battaglia, said, "What we want to do most of all is close out these cases and forget them. You are Kristofor Agbadashian, then?"

"Yes," Kristofor said, "although, as you know, I have been using another name—Charles Abbott—for about ten years. I had always had in mind making the change in any case, as my true name is difficult for the American tongue, and my maternal grandfather's name was Ahpet, which is very nearly the same as Abbott."

"Yes, that's sensible," Battaglia said. "A case of amnesia, would you say?"

"No," Kristofor said. "It wasn't amnesia. I hid, in my own house, because I didn't want to go. I knew what I was doing. My mother and my sisters begged me every day to give myself up and go into the Army, but I refused. I haven't for-gotten any of it. There has been no amnesia. And my life has proven itself too well for me to feel embarrassed about, or ashamed of, it. In my hometown I'm still remembered by a handful of very decent people as Kristofor Under the Bed. I am beginning to tell my kids about it, too. So far they think it's very funny."

"I understand," Battaglia said. "Under this line, Cause of Failure to Present Self, I have been putting down Amnesia, in case anybody takes it into his head to examine these forms, which isn't very likely. What do you suggest I put on your form?"

"Coward," Kristofor said.

"That would be as inaccurate as Amnesia," Battaglia said. He wrote in the space, and said, "Father. That'll do it, I'm sure. The case is closed." He left the shop, as if he had gone in to buy something and hadn't seen anything that suited him.

Cowards are nice, they're interesting, they're gentle, they wouldn't think of shooting down people in a parade from a tower. They want to live, so they can see their kids. They're very brave.

1974

Najari Levon's
Old Country Advice
to the Young Americans
on
How to Live with a Snake

NAJARI LEVON WENT TO ARAM'S HOUSE on Van Ness Avenue
for some legal advice about a private matter, but Aram hadn't
come home yet, so the old man with the gargoyle face was
asked to make himself at home somewhere.

He saw Aram's two small sons and two small daughters
on the linoleum floor of a glassed-in porch, playing a board
game and keeping score on a small pad with a small pencil,
and so he went there and sat down to watch.

A metal arrow at the center of the large board was spun,
and if it stopped in the space where there was a picture of a
bright star, for instance, the player was given ten points, but
just beside the picture of the star, there was a space in which
there was a picture of a small green snake, and if the needle

stopped there, ten points were taken away from the player's score.

The scorekeeper was Aram's firstborn, a boy of ten or eleven.

"Star," Aram's secondborn, a daughter, said, but the scorekeeper told his sister the needle was on the *line,* and *nearer* to the snake than to the star.

"Snake," he said, picking up the small pencil to put the score on the pad. His sister knocked the pad and pencil out of his hand, saying, "Star." And they began to fight.

Najari Levon said in Armenian, "In our house in Bitlis lived a very large black snake, which was our family snake."

The fighters stoped to listen, and he said, "No proper family was without its proper snake. A house was not complete without a snake, because the long snake crawling back of the walls held the house together."

The fighters relaxed, and he said, "Our snake had great wisdom. It was the oldest house snake in Bitlis."

The scorekeeper sprawled belly down on the floor, not far from the corner of the room where the small pencil had fallen during the fight.

"Did you see the snake?" he said.

The storyteller glanced at the small green pencil and then at the boy, and he said, "Yes, I saw the snake. His door into the house was at the top of the stone wall in the room where I slept, a door just big enough for the snake to pass through, about the size of a saucer. In the evening as soon as I got into my bed, I looked up at the snake's door, and there I would see him looking down at me."

"How much of him would you see?"

"Only the head, because it was nighttime now, and he would soon go to sleep, too."

"Did you ever see *all* of him?"

"Oh, yes."

"How big was he?"

"As big around as a saucer, with a very sensitive face, very large eyes—not the little eyes of English people, but the large eyes of Armenian people. And Kurdish people. And a very thoughtful mouth, like the mouth of John D. Rockefeller, but of course with a different kind of tongue, although I can't be sure of this, because I have seen in a newspaper only a picture of John D. Rockefeller, but not a picture of his tongue."

"Did you see the snake's tongue?"

"Many times, in and out, like words, but of course in his own language, not ours."

"How long was he?"

"Ten times the length of a walking stick. He was not small."

"What would he do back there?"

"He lived there. His house was on that side of the stone wall, our house was on our side. But of course there was no such thing as his and ours. The whole house was ours and the whole house was his, but he *lived* back of the wall. In the wintertime I would not see him, and I would almost forget he was there. And then one evening in the springtime I would look up at his door, and there he would be again. He would speak, but I would say, 'Not now, because it's night and time to sleep, but in the morning come down and I will bring you something to eat.' So in the morning . . ."

"What did he eat?"

"Milk. In the morning I filled a bowl with milk—not one of those little bowls soup is served in for a small man, but one of those large bowls for a large man. My mother asked where I was taking the bowl of milk, and I said, " 'Mama, I am taking the bowl of milk to the snake.' Everybody in our family, every man, every woman, and every child comes to my room to see the snake, because to have a snake in a house is baracat.* Everybody stands in the room and waits to see the snake. Thirty-three men, women, and children, instead of thirty-four, because during the winter my grandfather Setrak died."

"Did the snake come out?" the boy sprawled on the floor said.

"I took the bowl of milk, and put it in the corner straight across from the snake's door so that all of the snake would be able to come out of the door, down the wall, and across the floor. And then the thirty-three of us would be able to see *all* of the snake, from the head with the mouth like John D. Rockefeller's mouth, and with the eyes that are not the little eyes of English people, but the large eyes of Armenian people, and Kurdish people. I put the bowl down and look up at the snake's door, but the snake is not there, so I speak to the snake, I say to him, 'Sevavor, I have put the bowl of milk on the floor in the corner of the room, so come out of your door and down the wall and across the floor and have something to eat; it is no longer wintertime, it is springtime.' "

"Did he come down?"

"The snake came to the door to see who it was who was speaking to him, he came to see, he came to see who it was, was it me or was it somebody else, so when he came to see, I

---

* "Baracat" is "good fortune" in Arabic.

said, 'Don't worry, Sevavor, it is me, Levon, your friend. I am
the one who is speaking, Najari Levon.' The snake looked at
me, and then he looked at each of the others in the room,
but he did not come down, the snake did not come down
because we had been thirty-four and now were thirty-three, so
the snake did not come down. I said, 'Sevavor, in the wintertime my grandfather Setrak died—that is why we are no
longer thirty-four, we are now only thirty-three, but two of the
wives are pregnant and in August we will be more than thirty-
four, we will be thirty-five, and if one of the wives has twins,
we will be thirty-six, and if both of the wives have twins, we
will be thirty-seven, the Najari people will be thirty-seven,
Sevavor, so come out of the door, and down the wall, and
across the floor to the bowl of milk in the corner.' "

"Did he?"

"Very slowly, like this, like my arm, the snake came out
of the door, slowly, down the wall, like this, one walking-stick
length of the black body like this, slowly, down the wall, two
walking-stick lengths, very hungry, very old, very wise, three
walking-stick lengths, very black, four lengths, five lengths,
six lengths, and now the snake's head is on the floor like this,
but his tail is still behind the wall, and all of the Najari people
are watching and waiting, and slowly the snake pushes himself
forward on the floor a little nearer to the bowl of milk in the
corner, seven lengths out of the door, seven lengths down the
wall, eight lengths, nine lengths, and now all thirty-three of
the Najari people are almost not breathing, to see better the
Najari snake, the snake of the Najari people, from the head to
the tail, and now there is only one more length. As soon as the
snake moves one more length toward the bowl of milk in the
corner, every man, woman, and child in the room will see *all*

of the snake of our house, of our family, of the Najari people. But the snake stops. With only one more length to go the black snake moving to the white bowl of milk in the corner stops."

"Why?" the boy said, and the storyteller said, "An old snake who does not see an old man in the springtime because the old man is dead, an old snake who does not see an old man he saw in the summertime, because in the wintertime the old man died, an old snake stops to think about a thing like that. I said, 'Sevavor, do not be unhappy about my grandfather Setrak who died in the cold of wintertime; it is good for an old man to go to sleep in the snow, it is good for him to go home; if nobody went to sleep, if nobody went home, the house would soon be crowded and there would not be food enough for everybody. Do not be sorry for the old man, he is asleep, he has gone home, go and have the milk I have put in the bowl for you.' "

"Did he go?"

"The snake did not move, the black snake with his head and two walking-stick lengths on the floor, and seven lengths up the wall, and one length behind the wall, did not move, because when my grandfather Setrak was born the snake saw him, and every year of Setrak's life the snake saw him, but now the old man was dead, and the snake was on his way to the bowl of milk in the corner, but the snake did not want to move any more and all of the Najari people did not want to breathe. I said, 'Sevavor, do not worry about the old man, he is home, he is asleep, he is a small boy again running in the meadows, go and have your milk.' And then the snake, slowly, like a big black snake with eyes not like the little eyes of English people . . ."

"Yes, yes," the boy said. "Don't stop."

The old storyteller glanced at the small stub of green pencil on the floor, and then back at the boy, directly this time, scaring him a little, and then in English he said, "Dat your pancil?"

At that moment Aram came in and said, "What is it, Levon?"

The old man got up and chuckled deeply in the manner for which he was famous all over Fresno, and he said, "Aram Sevavor, I came for advice about a private matter. I came all the way from my house on L Street to your house on Van Ness Avenue, past the place where they have those red fire engines, all the way up Eye Street, where the police have their building, all the way up Forthcamp Avenue, I came, Aram Sevavor, one foot after the other, from my house to your house, I came, and now I go, I go all the way back, Aram Sevavor, because I can't remember the question I came to ask."

He went out the back, and down the alley, and the boy with the green pencil stood in the alley and watched him go, taking with him forever the end of the story about the snake.

1971

Mystic Games

WHEN OUR FAMILY LIVED IN ARMENIA, the long snowed-in winters of Bitlis impelled the invention of a game called My Mind, which frequently started in October and didn't end until the following April. When we came to America, the custom of the game came with us.

This is how it went: A player was supposed to say "My mind" (in Armenian, *Mytkus*) after he had accepted something, anything at all, such as a glass of water, from his opponent. But if one of the players accepted something from the other and did not say, "My mind," the other player, by saying, "*Yahdahst*," became the winner.

Frequently, a game could be started early in the evening and won in a matter of two or three hours. The rules of the game permitted trickery of any kind. To win at My Mind was a mark of wit. Kids were encouraged to take on adults, to sharpen their minds in an inexpensive way, as nothing more than pride was at stake, although now and then famous players played for other stakes; a ready-made suit from Yezdan's, for instance, or a five-dollar gold piece.

My uncle, Shag Bashmanian, the lawyer, was one of the best players of the game in the family. He frequently had

83

games going with eight or nine people at the same time. Upon receiving anything from the hand of anybody at all, he automatically said, "*Mytkus*," which frequently puzzled a bailiff in a courtroom who had just handed him Exhibit A. Consequently, the very first time he took me on, in the parlor of our house on O Street, he was shocked when I won the game so readily.

The winning of the game wasn't difficult at all. I was nine years old. I sold the *Evening Herald* after school every day, sometimes bringing home a dollar profit for household expenses, although most of the time I felt satisfied if I managed to earn half a dollar. That night I had gone home with forty cents and two leftover copies of the paper.

I had had a good supper of sour cabbage stew, and I was feeling pretty good when Shag drove up in his Apperson Jackrabbit, came into the house, and began to tell the latest chapter in the endless saga of his adventures.

Feeling too good to care about manners, I interrupted him to say, "I think I can beat you at My Mind."

He was so amazed that he burst into laughter, even while he shouted, "Who are you to challenge me? The greatest players have never fooled me. How can you?" And then, as if to teach me a very quick lesson, he said, "Very well, then, the game is on. This afternoon, as I was saying before you interrupted me, I called on Yezdan at his store and, taking a silver dollar out of my pocket, I asked him to guess the date on it, because if he guessed right I would hand him not one silver dollar, but ten."

As he spoke, Shag brought a silver dollar out of his pocket, looked at the date, and then said, "My game with

Yezdan is now in its seventh month, and so, of course, I wanted to win and get it over with. I couldn't help noticing that while Yezdan seemed to be interested in this strange offer I had just made, it wasn't very likely that he had forgotten the game, so I said to his son, 'Ara, please hold this dollar for a moment.' " And now Shag reached out to me with the dollar, as if I were Ara. I said, "*Mytkus*," and accepted the dollar. Shag was surprised, but not surprised enough to stop telling his story, which was long and funny. I laughed, as everybody else did, and handed the silver dollar to my brother, who looked at the date and said, "Eighteen seventy-four." This interruption provoked Shag into a rage that was better than half bogus, solely to scare me into forgetting the game.

"What kind of a family is this?" he shouted. "First, the little brother, and then the big brother interrupts me. But then this is the New World, isn't it? Everybody is the equal of everybody else in this world, isn't he? Well, maybe it's better to forget the old country, and the old-country rules of behavior. We are now Americans, every one of us. Let us therefore behave like Americans. I have always believed that it was brilliant of the Americans to answer the arrows and tomahawks of the wild Indians with glass beads for the women, whiskey for the men, and Christian charity for the children. You boys are children. Let me, therefore, show you a little Christian charity." He handed my brother a penny, and my brother said nothing, and then very quickly handed me one, too, but as I took it, I said, "*Mytkus*," and he pretended not even to have heard.

Shag continued to tell his story, waiting for another opportunity to trick me, and I decided how I would trick him. Before me on the round table were the two unsold copies of the *Evening Herald*. I began to look at the front page, and then, when Shag had come to the end of his story, I read from the front page loud enough for everybody to hear: " 'Pershing Says War Near End.' " And then, " 'Local Attorney Opens Office in Rowell Building. Recent graduate of the law school at the University of Southern California, Arshag Bashmanian'—hey, this story's about you."

Shag leaped to the table, seized the paper, and said, "Where? Where?"

"*Yahdahst*," I said, "that's where."

"There is no story in the paper about me?" Shag said.

"No, and there isn't about me, either, but there ought to be, because I just beat you at My Mind."

"It wasn't a real game," Shag said. "*This* will be a real game, so it must be for something."

"All right, let it be for the penny you just gave me," I said.

He stayed at our house another two hours, during which time he tried unsuccessfully six times to trick me, and then I pretended to fall alseep.

"Go to bed," my mother said to my brother and me. "Both of you."

My brother shook me. I pretended to wake up, acting more than half asleep as I got to my feet, and so Shag came to hand me something, but instead of taking it I bent down, pretending to pick something off the rug on the floor, and then I said, "You must have dropped this gold piece," and I handed him his penny, again saying, "*Yahdahst*."

He was crazy about himself, and about money, and I'd got him on both.

After that, everything I ever told him about himself or about money he considered very carefully, even if we didn't have a game going.

1967

Twenty Is the Greatest Time in Any Man's Life

"WELL, SIT DOWN, then, at least," the father said, "and take it easy, take your time, I'm in no hurry, I've got all the time in the world, you don't have to rush into any of it, don't talk at all for a minute or two, I'll get you a cup of coffee."

"Well, I suppose you know," the son said, "because every time I want to talk to you, something's wrong, so I suppose you know something's wrong."

"We'll see what it is and don't worry about it," the father said, "because no matter what it is, what could it be? This Horn and Hardart Instant Coffee I think you'll like. With canned milk I can get a cup of coffee just like the one that comes out of the spout at the Automat, and sometimes even a better cup, because now and then but not too often the coffee out of the spout at the Automat goes a little bad."

"I get a big kick out of the way you take a lot of your meals at the Automat," the son said, "when everybody else I

know goes to Sardi's or some place like that. You don't go to
the Automat to save money, do you, Pop?"

"I don't mind saving money, but I go because I like the
guck they have there, and there's no fuss to it. I really don't
enjoy a lot of fuss about getting a little food down the gullet
and into the gut. I've done it all; it doesn't make me proud or
happy when I'm not kept waiting at a fancy restaurant and
I'm given a good table and the waiters call me by name; it
gives me a pain, it embarrasses me."

"Why should it? You're entitled to it. Why not enjoy
your fame and success the way everybody else does?"

"I did in fact enjoy it when it was new, but how long is
any man entitled to enjoy something so really silly? How about
that coffee?"

"It's the best cup of coffee I think I've ever had," the
son said.

"I drink two or three cups at a time three or four times
a day," the father said. "I think the cost comes to less than
two cents a cup, and as you know at the Automat it's a dime.
That makes me feel good."

"Why does saving eight cents a cup mean so much to
you?"

"It isn't just the eight cents. The coffee's *here*, and I
don't have to go out and look for the nearest Automat. But
the eight cents saved pleases me, too. When I'm working I
get a kick out of getting by on as little money as I got by on
when I was just starting out. I have this idea that it helps the
work, and I actually believe it does."

"But the rent on this penthouse is more than twenty-five
dollars a day," the son said, "so what good is saving sixty or
seventy cents a day on coffee?"

"I save about *fifty* dollars a day on meals and booze and taxis," the father said. "I *walk* everywhere I happen to go, you know, and with the saving on coffee it all mounts up. The penthouse isn't a luxury, though; it's my office. Only so far the joint vibrates all day from the heating and ventilating motors just overhead, and there are always a lot of stupid noises from the motors that I don't enjoy at all. And so, having leased the place for three years seems to have the makings of a great big fat mistake, but I've been assured that the vibrations and the noises are going to stop. I took the place because I've got to live and work and conduct my business, such as it is, somewhere, and when this building was unfinished this place up here overlooking the United Nations Building and the East River seemed pretty good. Rent at a third-rate hotel these days is around fifteen dollars a day for one lousy room, and I've had it, I thought I ought to have a place of my own for a change. It isn't working, though."

"Twenty-five dollars a day for three years is more than a dollar an hour night and day," the son said.

"Yes. I've figured it all out on a piece of paper, and I really think I goofed. So what do you do when you goof? You see if you can make the thing work out, after all, and of course that's why I'm trying to work, although the going is bad, on account of the vibrations and noise all the time."

"Can't you stop working, and just forget everything?"

"No, I can't. I owe too much money, and there are three legal actions various people have brought against me, and whatever the outcome of these actions may be, they are going to cost money—for lawyers to begin with, and then to satisfy the demands of the actions themselves. I'm caught, I've got to work. I don't mind, work is the only thing I really know or care about in any case. I only hope the work goes on being worth money because if it isn't there isn't any other way for me to get any money. You'll be twenty soon and you'll be getting involved in the whole business, and you'll understand about these things. I'm going to have another cup; let me make another for you, too."

"O.K., and thanks," the son said. "And while you're making them, maybe I'd better start telling you the bad news."

"O.K.," the father said, "but whatever the hell it is, don't worry about it; don't be afraid I'm going to flip my lid about it, and even if I do, don't let that bother you too much, either. I've known you from your first hour, and apart from the inevitable feeling I have for you, as my son, whatever that means, I've always been fascinated by your nature, your character, your identity, your style, and all of the rest of it. I'd really like you to be who you are, who you most want to be, and I'd like things to go nicely for you."

"Well, that's just it, maybe," the son said. "Things aren't going nicely for me, I'm probably who I am, whoever it is, but I don't know about who I most want to be, or how to become whoever that is, either. I mean, I've quit college again, only this time I *haven't* quit, I've been flunked out. I thought I handed in a very good paper in psychology, but the guy gave me a failing mark because he said I hadn't answered the question. You remember the paper. That started it. I guess I believed in that paper so much that when he flunked me I couldn't believe I could make it in any of the subjects, and so I didn't. That's two colleges in one year. Everybody's angry at me, I've had some bad arguments, I've been called names, and I've called people a few names myself. I thought I'd better come and tell you about it."

"I'm glad you did, I'm glad you did."

"I guess the trouble is I'm not sure the people who are angry at me aren't right. Phil's a good guy, but anyhow my mother's married to him, so anything he says she says, too, and he says I've got about as much backbone as a jellyfish, and you know how my mother is when the atmosphere gets ugly, she gives me ultimatums, and so last night when Phil was hollering at me and I was hollering back at him, she told me to apologize or get out. I mean, I phoned from Mike Shepard's a little while ago, where I spent the night. She told me to get out, so I went, only I haven't got any money, and didn't brush my teeth this morning because I didn't take a toothbrush, even. I hate to bring you this kind of stupid bad news all the time, but I don't want to impose on Mike Shepard's mother who insists I must stay at her house."

"Well, I've got a hundred dollars in my wallet," the father said, "and I can get more as you need it, or I can get you a thousand if you happen to need it to get yourself into a small apartment. I'm not asking you to stay here because I don't want to put you in the position of feeling you've got to, and I know you would rather not. We tried it two or three times and it never worked."

"I'm sorry I've goofed again," the son said.

"I don't think you've *goofed*, necessarily. It all depends on what use you make of whatever it is that's going on. It is not absolutely necessary for you to go to college, because you are not interested in becoming something—like a lawyer or a doctor or a teacher or an engineer or something—that you can't become unless you do go to college. If you've decided that what you want to do is paint, paint. If it's to write, write. If it's do nothing for a while, do nothing for a while, although

I have the idea that at twenty a man is lucky if he knows what he wants to do, and luckier if it doesn't happen to be to do nothing, even for a while. It's very hard to do nothing. The people who do nothing, by choice, or because they can't make a decision, or because they can't seem to get started doing what they really want to do, they go bad, they get into trouble! Doing nothing is no fun at all, and sooner or later it makes some kind of zombie out of a man."

"Why a zombie?" the son said.

"I don't know," the father said, "but maybe it's because he gets to feeling sorry for himself and decides the only thing to do is some marijuana, hanging around with the rest of the boys who aren't doing anything and are feeling sorry for themselves, because *they're* smoking marijuana, or trying junk, getting themselves all worked up and weaker and weaker but thinking all the time they're getting stronger and stronger. I'd certainly rather not see you become a zombie. Zombies have got to do a lot of hanging around together—weaklings, liars, cheaters. Everybody respects them these days, everybody thinks that if they don't respect them it means they're against civil liberties or something, but I can only *sympathize* with them a little, but only a little; I can't respect them, they bore me—their everlasting bawling about their tricky little sadnesses and deprivations of childhood bore me. You've introduced me to some of the people you know. I don't dislike any of them, but I really can't pretend I believe in any of them, or that they don't bore me. And in being critical of them of course I'm being critical of you, too, at least for having them as friends. There are other people around, too, you know, not just the ones who start by giving up, and then just hang around to see what giving up leads to. It leads to being a zombie of one sort or another."

"I'm not a zombie, am I?" the son said.

"No, of course you're not," the father said, "but I don't get the impression you think enough of yourself to make demands on yourself that aren't easy, and that's the quickest way there is to begin to be a zombie. I've always tried to keep myself from telling you how it was with me when I was your age because I didn't want to impose myself on you, but now I think I'd better tell you. I thought I was potentially one of the best, ever, at anything, and that I was O.K. right now. And I think that that's a better attitude for a young man to have about himself than the attitude that he isn't O.K. Quitting college is just right if you know what you want to do instead, and want to give it a good honest try; but already I'm doing all the talking, and try as I will I can't keep it from being another lecture of another father to another son. I'm glad you quit. I want to do anything I can for you, even though you and I both know that having somebody do something for us is actually the worst thing for us—money, talk, or anything else, like praying, for instance."

"It's not as serious as that, is it, Pop?"

"You know, and I don't," the father said. "For yourself, I mean. I know how it is for me, how it had been from the beginning for me, how it was along the way, how it is now, and how it has got to be tomorrow. I have got to make my way, I've got to earn it. Nobody can help me. If I can't help myself, good-bye, Joe, as the saying is. You're not too young to get to work at this. We've had some bad arguments about it, and while I don't want you not to say your say, I don't want to be in the position of finding fault with the way you think you can do whatever it is you think you want to do. I don't want to find fault simply because you give me no choice, and that's how it is when you argue for your right not to demand any-thing tough of yourself. Well, it's got to be tough, period— except of course for the unfortunates I've mentioned, who soon enough have it tougher than anybody else, in any case. And I know everything I'm saying is useless; it doesn't do you any good; God knows it does me none at all, but I just haven't got any choice. You tell me what to tell you, or tell me any-thing. Not for me, tell me for yourself. What can I tell you, except the stupid little I know? The crazy little that was right for me, and worked for me? I don't know anything else. Do you dig anything I'm saying?"

"I dig it *all*," the son said. "I haven't decided what I want to do."

"Well, maybe it's all right for you not to decide for a while longer," the father said. "No two people crack a walnut, even, in the same way, let alone anything else. I'm sorry, don't let anything I've said bother you too much; I guess it's just that I still can't help worrying about you; I'm going to shut up now and go out on the terrace and look down at the side-walk and out at the East River. Stick around. Go brush your teeth—you'll find some new brushes and shaving stuff in the second bathroom. Shave too if you feel like it, take a bath, take a nap if you feel like it, feel at home, because the fact is that I thought maybe when I signed the lease for this place you might want to come and have your own room and bath and share the joint; but it's all right, I won't crowd you. There's the money. I'll get you as much more as you want. We're both smoking one cigarette after another, not getting through most likely, trying to make it but not making it. I don't know what goes on with you, and I can't make any clearer than I've been trying to most of your life what I think about you, how much I think of you, how highly; but it isn't enough, it isn't really any of my business. I'd rather you had a purpose, even if it made a square of you. I'm glad you're not a square, but I can't be glad that it doesn't come to anything more than only that. I am a square. You see, I believe in myself, just as I always have. If you're not here when I come back from the terrace, it's all right; just phone me any time, come by, or not, everything will be just fine, don't worry about it. One thing more, maybe the most important thing, is this. Are you in the bathroom? Well, anyway, what I was going to say is twenty is the greatest time in any man's life. I hope it's being great for you."

1977

How the Barber Finally Got Himself into a Fable

THERE WAS ONCE A BARBER who visited a fabulist and said, "Sir, you are not writing enough fables about barbers."

"Who, for instance?" the fabulist said, putting down his hammer and chisel, for he was writing on stone.

"Well," the barber said, "*me*, because I am the barber who thought up the complaint, and I want you to say that I am Betros of Gultik and am very brave."

"What else?" the fabulist said.

"I do all the good things for men that all barbers do," the barber said, "and then I do something no other barber does."

"And what is that?" the fabulist said.

"Do you promise to put me into a fable?" the barber said.

"No, but I think you ought to tell me just the same," the fabulist said.

"Very well, then," the barber said. "The thing I do that other barbers do not do is this. I speak wisdom to my customers."

"Give me an example of the wisdom you speak," the fabulist said.

"I say to them," the barber said, " 'Do not laugh out loud at a cripple.' "

"I see," the fabulist said.

"Are you going to put me in a fable?" the barber said.

"No, I don't think so," the fabulist said.

The barber said, "Why not? I am not laughing at you and you are a cripple—your back is all hunched up, your legs can scarcely support your little body, your head is lopsided, your fingers are so twisted nobody can look at them for longer than a glance. I am not laughing, so why aren't you going to put me in a fable?"

"Well," the fabulist said, "if you really want to know the truth, it is this: I would much rather have you laugh at me than ask that I put you into a fable."

The barber pointed a finger. He leaped back in rage. He roared with mock laughter. "Look, look," he said, "everybody look at this deformed little monkey of a man who claims to be a fable-writer, he is a fraud, that's what he is—naturally, being deformed, he had to learn *some* trade, so he chose the easiest one in the world."

The fabulist looked and listened, and then said softly, "Now, perhaps I may put you in a fable, after all. It is more right for some people to be honest monsters than it is for them to be unsuccessful toadies."

1977

There Was a
Young Lady of Perth

I sold the first issue of *Liberty* magazine. In it was the beginning of the memoirs of George M. Cohan, and a limerick contest, for which the first prize was an enormous sum of money. Was it five thousand dollars, fifty thousand, or five hundred thousand? In any case, it was enough to make me stop and think about there having been a young lady of Perth.

Now, of course, I'm not unaware that most people don't remember the first issue of *Liberty* magazine, if in fact they remember the second. How could they? The magazine saw the light of day when I was not much more than eleven or twelve, or thirteen or fourteen.

Did I sell it, or did I buy it? Did I make a profit of two and a half cents, or did I throw away a nickel? Memory fails me, and while it's not as bad as if a bank had failed me, it's bad enough, because I *deal* in memory. And when memory fails me, I'm in trouble. I have either got to invent, or I have got to do research.

I can invent fair to middling, feeling an awful liar all the while, but I can't do research worth a bottle cap. I forget what I'm looking for and wind up with six or seven other things that I can't use. I don't mind inventing if there is a little aesthetic truth in it, as we say in the profession—"versimilitude," I once heard one writer say, but I can't vouch for either the spelling or the aptness. Very *similar* would have to be the words I would use, because I can spell those words and believe I know what they mean.

George M. Cohan happened to be a man I admired even more than I admired Benjamin Franklin, who was quite simply one of the truly great cutups in my life, as of course (later on, and in a different way) George M. Cohan was. I knew Ben had put up a kite and taken a chance on electrocution in order to invent electricity, and I knew he had written a boy's story called *The Autobiography of*, but the thing I liked about him was his easygoing way of getting to be a great man. Finally, they sent him to Paris as the ambassador, and he *enchanted* the French, in their own words.

And so, in that first issue of *Liberty* magazine I was eager to find out how George M. Cohan had begun his life, because George, the Yankee Doodle Dandy, was still alive and kicking. I thought it would be interesting to find out his secret of success, in case someday our paths were to cross. There was no such chance with Ben Franklin, of course.

Was the year 1924? If so, Ben had been dead for some time, and George M. was surely not much more than thirty. Or might it have been forty? Thirty or forty, he was certainly at the height of his fame, writing plays, singing, dancing, and being an all-round American Boy, born on Independence Day. They made a movie about him, but I presumed they had done it for money, so I never saw it.

The world was different then, whether it was 1924, or a couple of years earlier, or a couple later. It was just plain different. It wasn't necessarily better, and in all probability it was worse, but an American Boy had a chance in those days, on his own, unsponsored, so to say. All he needed was willingness, wit, and vitality, and so it was great to be an American, to be under voting age, to be unknown, to have the challenge there night and day, still unmet.

Liberty magazine had a fine editorial policy, although I have forgotten precisely what it was. In the name of something, somebody meant to be an American Boy, and to make money. I envied him, although I didn't know his name. He was back of the whole thing, though, and the arrival of his magazine into my life was an event of some importance.

After work, I examined the magazine from cover to cover to find out what it came to, and then I read George M. Cohan's contribution, which I found fascinating, because he was swift, confident, and talented. He was born backstage, and as soon as he could walk he went out and wowed 'em, singing, dancing, and telling jokes.

The photographs of George and his beautiful sister and his handsome father and mother were an inspiration, but in those days the theater wasn't my line, and so if I was to get started in the business of making my fame and fortune, out of the pages of Liberty magazine, it would have to be by winning the limerick contest, by making something out of the fact that there was a young lady of Perth, if in fact that was what it was, as it probably wasn't, although it was certainly the equivalent of it.

The trouble was I didn't know anything about limericks, but Liberty magazine gave a brief history of them, how they had originated in a place called Limerick, and the magazine also gave three or four illustrations of perfect ones. These were

incredibly clever, apt, wise, and witty. Somebody from somewhere tried to do something and as a result something unexpected happened. In a way, that was a little like the story of
my life up to that time, and now it was time for a change.
Instead of being the subject of a limerick, I wanted to be a
writer of one, I wanted to be the writer of the greatest limerick
of all time, because that would mean that I would win the
contest, I would win the money, and people would say, "There
goes the American Boy who wrote the limerick."

I couldn't think of a second line, though. There was a
young lady of Perth; who she was or what she was up to, I
couldn't guess.

I kept it in mind, though. I had the first line, supplied
by the magazine, and all I needed next was a second line that
was so extraordinary that the rest of the lines of the limerick
would fall into place and sound like perfection itself. The
words that rhymed with Perth were "worth," "mirth," "birth,"
"dearth," "girth," and, of course, "earth"—all good usable
words. There was a birth, there were mirth and worth and the
others, and so all I really needed to do was rattle them together
and throw them out like dice, for a natural. With my conscious mind, the mind that was supposed to be equal to such
a challenge, equal to thought, I had little luck. "There was a
young lady of Perth who didn't know what she was worth,"
for instance, just wasn't right.

And so I slept on it, or, to be a little more exact, it slept
on me. The young lady of Perth was here, there, and everywhere, but the limerick remained incomplete, and I woke up in
the morning knowing I had been in a fight and hadn't won.

•   •   •

That first issue of *Liberty* magazine passed from me to my brother, who also took an interest in the limerick contest, and then to my sisters, so that before the second issue of the magazine came out everybody in my family was at work trying to win fame and fortune as a limerick writer. We weren't good at it, though. I don't know who fell out first, but I know it wasn't me. I think it was my brother, who tended to be cynical about contests in general, and about theories of how easy it is to rise in the world. He said it just wasn't an overnight proposition. A man of thirteen, he believed, was a little less likely to be invited to Washington to discuss educational reform with President Harding than a man of sixteen, for instance. But a man of sixteen was less likely than a man of nineteen, and our neighborhood was pretty well stocked with nineteen-year-old American Boys who knew a thing or two about educational reform—throw out teachers who had remained stupid after considerable schooling. That was the basic educational reform principle of the neighborhood.

I noticed with regret my brother's scorn for the limerick-writing contest, and I made up my mind to be different. I made up my mind to have stick-to-itiveness, because I had heard that everybody who had ever amounted to anything had had stick-to-itiveness. I reasoned that if *they* had had it and had *needed* it, and had won through to success on *account* of it, I was going to have it, too. Every evening when I got home from work I checked with the other contestants, only to discover, after two or three such checks, that everybody had given up. I also discovered that my persistence, or stick-to-itiveness, was being taken for a nuisance.

Somebody said, "To hell with the young lady of Perth. This is Fresno."

This amounted to nothing better than the waving of the white flag, surrender, armistice, failure, humiliation. I was flabbergasted and more determined than ever to win the contest.

There was time, the deadline was still ten or eleven days off, and I felt confident that long before the required midnight postmark of the final day I would have my limerick neatly written and on its way to *Liberty* magazine in—wherever it was. I don't believe it was in New York, or in Chicago, either. I just don't remember where it was, but it was somewhere, and this place could be reached by train mail in a matter of six or seven days. There was no airmail in those days.

One afternoon the chain on my bike broke while I was sprinting, and I was sent over the handle bars onto the pavement. Something was always happening to my bike. It wasn't holding up, but nobody ever said, "They don't make them the way they used to." The wire spokes of the wheel were always loosening, and while I had a spoke tightener, as every practical-minded messenger had, whenever I tightened a couple of loose spokes I noticed that the alignment of the wheel became unbalanced. You had to be an expert even in a thing like that.

The dive was on my head, which was at least a little protected by the blue cap of Postal Telegraph, or at any rate would have been had the cap not fallen off just before my head struck the pavement, when I needed it most.

It was quite a jolt, but, as always, I hoped there had been no witnesses, for I despised having accidents, and I resented help and sympathy.

The minute my head hit the pavement the whole winning limerick came to me, and I was stunned by the brilliance and rightness of it, the simplicity and inevitability of it, and by the fact that it had taken a foolish accident to bring the thing around. I was all set to begin committing it to memory before I forgot it when an elderly lady of Fresno hurried up and asked, as a mother or a grandmother might, "Are you all right?"

"Yes, ma'am, it's nothing, thank you." All quickly said, so she would be satisfied and move along, but no, she wanted to chat.

"Are you sure? Here, let me help you up."

Well, then I realized I was still flat on my back, so I leaped to my feet, picked up the fallen bike, and began to unwheel the chain, which had become entangled around the hub.

There was no getting away from her, or rather no getting her away from me. On and on she chatted, and of course my upbringing compelled me to answer every question respectfully.

At last I was able to walk away with my bike. It was time to commit the limerick to memory, but all I could remember was the first line again. The thing was lost.

I was still so mad that evening when I got home that my brother couldn't help noticing.

"What's the matter with you?"

"Lousy chain broke again."

I didn't want to tell him about the limerick because I was afraid he wouldn't believe me, and a younger brother hates not being believed. I'd *had* that whole limerick right after I had dived, and it was the winning one, too. I'd had it, and then that nice old lady of Fresno had come up and had made me forget it. My brother examined by head and told me there was a bump there. I told him I *knew* there was a bump there. He wasn't really satisfied with my reason for being mad, and little by little he won me over to a full confession. I was astonished that he *didn't* disbelieve me. On the contrary, he was sure that I *had* had the winning limerick and had lost it.

"The thing to do," he said, "is to get it back."

"How?"

"The same way."

"Sprint and break the chain and dive on my head? Nothing doing."

"That's how it came to you. That's how you'll get it back. If you want something badly enough, you've got to pay the price for it."

"It was an accident," I said. "I'm not going to have an accident on purpose. I don't think it's possible in the first place, and even if it were, even if I *had* another accident, how do I know what kind of limerick I'd get out of it? It might not be the winner at all."

"Suit yourself," my brother said.

Now, it never occurred to me that he was having fun, and I kept thinking about his suggestion. After supper we went out to the back yard, where our wheels were. I looked at mine, with the chain as good as new again, repaired by Frank the Portuguese bike man, from whom we had bought our bikes, secondhand, and after a moment I got on the bike real slow and easy and rode out across the empty lot adjoining our back yard, and then out onto the sidewalk of San Benito Avenue, and then out onto the pavement of M Street, and there I began to sprint. My brother came running after me, shouting, "For God's sake, I was only kidding, don't do it, you'll kill yourself."

Well, the fact is I really hadn't *meant* to do it, I had only meant to sprint, racing, going as fast as I could go, as a kind of test of the fates. The chain was strong, and it just wasn't likely to break—unless the fates wanted me to take another dive, get back the winning limerick, and be on my way to fame and fortune. I heard my brother. The memory of what it was I had a lot of—stick-to-itiveness—came back to me, and I decided I *would* do my best to make that repaired chain snap and break, after all. I raced three blocks to Ventura Avenue without luck; the chain was as strong as ever. My brother rode up on his wheel and said, "Now, look, if you really think that that's the way to get the lost limerick back, I'll do everything I can to help you."

"How?"

"I'll hold you about two feet above the pavement—that's enough—and drop you. It's safer that way."

We were riding back on M Street in any case, so we rode on up to the Rainier Brewery, a kind of Bavarian red-brick castle entangled in railroad tracks and company roads, and we rode around the brewery, closed now, finished for the day, and we discussed the problem. After a while we dismounted and sat on the steps of the brewery to discuss procedure a little further and to make sure that nobody was around. The coast was clear and procedure had been agreed upon, when Eddie Imirian and Johnny Suni came up, bouncing an old tennis ball. My brother and I were challenged to a game of handball against the brewery wall. We won 21 to 18, and then it was dark, but Eddie and Johnny wanted another game, so we played in the dark and won 21 to 12.

When we reached our house, the boys sat with us on our front porch steps and talked about school. It looked as if they never wanted to go home, but finally they did, and my brother said, "Well, how about it?"

"The tar on San Benito Avenue isn't hard enough," I said.

"Want to try the sidewalk?"

"It's *harder* than the pavement I hit."

"Whatever you say."

Well, we were both pretty tired, but it seemed to me this was a matter of stick-to-itiveness if I ever saw one, so I quickly said, "Let's try her."

My brother was holding me around the knees, about two feet over the sidewalk, and was all set to drop me on my head when my mother came out on the front porch with a pitcher of tahn on a tray. "Oh-oh," my brother said.

Well, it was now or never, so I said, "Let's go."

Now, I was all set to get back the winning limerick, but my brother didn't let go.

"Why are you holding your brother that way?" my mother said.

"Just exercise," my brother said. "We take turns."

He let me down, and I took him around the knees and held him precisely as he had held me. For a moment I thought of dropping *him*, without plan, but I thought better of it and didn't.

"Come and drink tahn," my mother said.

I let him down and we went up onto the porch and drank two big glasses each of the best drink in the world. Put two cups of yogurt in a pitcher, add four or five cups of cold water, stir, and drink.

Well, the drink was great, because it helped you to know how alive you were, and what a privilege it was.

One of my sisters began to play *Dardanella* on the piano, and the other began to sing. My brother and I listened and looked around at where we were, and then up at the sky, full of stars. It was kind of silly, in a way, living in a house like that, nothing to it really, a few boards and a little wallpaper, and us, in a whole neighborhood like that, but what could you do? The tahn was great. The air was full of something that made you know you were alive, and the sky seemed a lot like something almost as good as money in the bank.

Pretty soon my sisters came out on the porch. We all sat around and talked and told jokes and laughed. I liked it, but I kept feeling I was losing my stick-to-itiveness, and that was the one thing I couldn't afford to lose. After about an hour we went inside to close up for the night.

My brother dropped me headfirst onto my bed, but all I did was bounce. The winning limerick didn't come back. And then I dropped him, and all *he* did was bounce.

I did my best with my conscious mind, and sent in a limerick, and lost.

I read every installment of George M. Cohan's life, and I envied him. I read the winning limerick, too. It didn't come to very much.

About forty years later I reached Perth, which is on the west coast of Australia. It seemed like a nice place, something like Fresno, I saw the young lady of Perth in person. I saw

her six or seven *hundred* times, as a matter of fact. I *spoke* to
her six or seven times. She replied in a nice Australian accent.
There was nothing suitable for a limerick in her.

She was just a nice girl.

In 1939 I met George M. Cohan in the offices of a
theater in New York. He was a gentle, kindly fellow with a
touch of sorrow in his eyes.

Liberty magazine changed hands a couple of times, and
then gave up the ghost.

I forgot all about limericks. Also, stick-to-itiveness.

I decided that *don't-stick-to-itiveness* is a pretty usable
philosophy, too, especially for a writer.

1961

How to Choose a Wife

MY ARMENIAN FAMILY, the Bashmanians, for all its fame for wit, speed, intelligence, worldliness, industry, thrift, practicality, humor, and wisdom, has always seemed to me stupid, especially when it comes to women.

Everybody in the family has always said, "God help the man who marries a Bashmanian girl," because if God doesn't help him, the girl certainly won't, and under the circumstances he couldn't possibly help himself. It isn't that the family is oversexed, although in comparison with many they are, or that it is undersexed, although no Bashmanian, male or female, has ever been a specialist at the business of male and female together. While nobody has ever neglected the sexual aspects of the human experience entirely, neither has anybody gone berserk about it. The family theory appears to have always been that a boy or man marries a girl at least ten years his junior solely for the purpose of establishing a home, founding a family, and getting a lot of kids out into the environment as quickly as possible, just in case, perhaps—just in case, that is, one of them at last is the right one.

As for a Bashmanian girl, the family theory has always been to get her out of the house before she is twenty, because an unmarried Bashmanian girl of twenty is impossible to live with, owing to the loud intelligence that constitutes for her the condition of being unmarried. Or would it be the loud responsibility? In any case, out of the house before the voice changes, or to prevent it from changing too much.

Old Hamazasp Bashmanian failed in that basic family principle with his last-born, called Hamazaspouhi, which is the feminine of his own given name, who at the age of twenty-two could look at a man, woman, child, or animal and foretell his, her, or its future. She was big, proud, loud, voluptuous, and clairvoyant. She insisted on shaking hands with everybody she met and invariably cracked their knuckles. Somebody gave her the nickname of The Halfback of Notre Dame, and even Hamazasp himself, when he heard it, did not protest.

She herself was inconsistent about how she should be addressed, saying one day, "Hamazaspouhi, pronounce each syllable clearly, it's my name," but on another day, perhaps to the same person, "Hamazasp is all you need to say. I am my father's daughter, not my mother's." Now and then, though, she said, "Hamazaspouhi is too long, Zasp is quite enough if said sharply." Or if she had been especially effective lately at clairvoyance she said, "Beloved of the Moon is my real name, or else how would I have ever predicted the Riff Riots? Everybody has a real name, given by nature itself. If you will hold still a moment and let me look at you clearly I will be glad to let you know what your real name is, since my relationship to nature is so close we are practically the same thing. Your real name is Fearless Running Rabbit."

This was a truck driver named Ashod Sevavorian, famous for his strength, who had been taken to meet the girl on the chance that he might just imagine he could learn to like her, as the saying is.

"Fearless? Running? Rabbit?" he said. "If the rabbit's fearless, what's he running for?"

"The meaning of one's real name is not always immediately clear, but I am sure it will come to you. A new meaning of my real name comes to me almost every day. Perhaps you are not aware that the rabbit was considered sacred and mystical by the ancient Adjemians."

"The ancient *who?*"

"Adjemians."

"Who are *they?*"

"Surely you have heard of the Adjemians of Fresno. They were once ancient. I was told by Makrouhi Adjemian herself how the rabbit was worshipped by her people."

"I thought you meant an ancient people like the Assyrians."

"Be proud of your name."

"I am."

"I don't mean Ashod Sevavorian. I mean your real name."

"Ashod Sevavorian is the only name I have, or want."

"May I ask your age, in that case?"

"Thirty-three."

"Just as I thought. Another misconception. Your real age is three thousand, three hundred and thirty-three."

The old man said, "Talk about cooking, housekeeping, and children. What good are real names and mystical numbers to a strong man and a handsome woman who might at any moment start a family?"

"Papa, everybody knows I cook everything, keep a clean house, and am adored by children."

"It's absolutely true," the old man said to the truck

driver. "Think twice before you permit appearances to deceive you into a negative decision."

The fact is that the truck driver had been powerfully moved by the sexual challenge of the girl—until she had started talking. Her eyes, her voice, her gestures, her smiles, her posture, everything about her was so ferociously sex-charged that he said to himself, "Who's got time for a fight like that?" But his decision had in fact long since been negative, not because she wasn't herself a Riff Riot in the bedroom, but because she obviously was, and the truck driver was trying to build up a business. If he ever went into a bedroom with her, he knew he wouldn't care to leave, and that would mean goodbye to the fleet of trucks he was sure he would own in two or three years.

He married a very ordinary girl with whom he shared a bed precisely eleven times in eleven years for eleven children, six boys and five girls, alternating. After the arrival of the eleventh, his sixth and last son, he owned and operated a fleet of sixty trucks and was one of the richest men in the whole San Joaquin Valley.

As for Beloved of the Moon, in her twenty-fourth year she began to be Beloved of Every Boy and Man who could put up with her talk and outwrestle her—up to a never-delayed point, after which the going was the best known to mortal man. And it was thus that she was happy to know the mystical experience, until it became imperative to make a choice of one, which she did, and six months later welcomed her first child, appropriately female. Her husband, a wine maker named Vahan Dulgarian, could scarcely be moved out of the house for three years, during which she bore three more daughters; then he died suddenly of obvious causes, whereupon the widow renounced the mystical experience in order to devote all of her time and energy to more mundane matters, like clairvoyance.

Most of the daughters of the Bashmanians, however, married sometime between sixteen and twenty, directed their husbands into miscellaneous careers, and brought up a variety of kids, each an interesting variation of the general Bashmanian character, at least partly mistakenly presumed to be brilliant, all of them without exception related by the very real characteristic of the family—stupidity.

Now and then Hamazasp Bashmanian came to my house to talk to somebody—anybody would do, just so it was somebody in the family, he didn't want too many outsiders to know what he knew—and so it came to pass that on several occasions he talked to me, since I was the only member of the family at home.

"You'll be eleven in a year or two," he said one day, "so perhaps it is not too early to bring up the matter of marriage."

"I'm eleven now, I'll be twelve in August, three months from now."

"I swear you look no older than eight or nine."

"It may be because I've got a fever. I've been ordered to stay home, but I refused to stay in bed, at any rate."

"An excellent principle, especially for a married man. Remember that, when you become a married man. I'm sure it's the fever that made me imagine you are only eight or nine. It does that, you know, especially the terrible fever that comes into a man the minute he settles down in his own house with his own wife, a total stranger. Well, since she's going to be in the house for a long time to come he wants her to stop being a stranger as quickly as possible, and so of course he spends a lot of time with her, and that is when the fever starts. No matter how much time he spends with her, the woman simply doesn't stop being a stranger. And so the fever doesn't stop, either. The whole purpose of the marriage is to found a family of course—anything else would be unthinkable—and so of course the children begin to arrive, but even after four of them, even after five, even after six, even after seven, which as you know is the number of children in my family, *have* arrived, the woman continues to be a stranger to the man, although to the children she is not a stranger. How could she be, since, whoever she is, she is their mother? It is simply impossible for him to understand the woman, and that is the thing I want to speak to you about. The reason the man can't understand the woman is that when he should have been most intelligent he was most stupid—when he first met her. Had he been intelligent he would have known that this was *not* the woman for him to marry, but because he had been stupid he had instantly believed that this was the *only* woman in the world to be his wife and the mother of his children. He went mad, in short. Bear that in mind when the time comes as of course it will before you know it. The English language has an expression our language doesn't have—something about falling in love. There is an element of falling in whatever it is they are talking about, but the fact is that what the expression really means is that a man has gone mad or has become seriously ill. In the founding of a family falling in love, as it's called, can only lead to a lifetime of sorrowful mistakes, and so this condition, this madness, this illness, you must try to avoid."

"How? I don't want to be mad, I hate to be sick, I don't want a lifetime of sorrowful mistakes."

. . .

The old man replied. "That is what I have taken an hour to walk here to tell you. How shall you avoid being overwhelmed by the first girl who seems overwhelmed by you, and by her very manner suggests that anything that interferes with the continuing of this overwhelming of one another is an unholy thing, and seems suddenly the most beautiful and exciting creature of her kind, who in turn clearly informs you without saying one word that you are the most handsome and wonderful creature of your kind, both of you going mad and becoming desperately ill. How shall you avoid this happening?"

"How?"

"First, go and meet her mother. If that doesn't banish your madness, and in nine cases out of ten it will, go and meet her mother's mother, if she's alive, and she generally is. Talk to her, because if you marry the daughter, you will soon enough be talking to the mother, and then to the grandmother, so you might as well know from the beginning what the talk is going to be like. If it's small talk, that's the kind of talk you're going to have to do the rest of your life."

"Suppose it's big talk?"

"Think twice about that, too, because it deserves to be thought about twice. Think twice about everything, and if it is at all possible think three times. Socrates thought four times about everything, but by then it was too late, his wife thought he was a bore."

"Three times if possible, preferably four, but *on time* instead of too late."

"Precisely. You will be expected to marry an Armenian girl. Don't do it."

"Why not?"

"It's bad enough being in the same house with a stranger the rest of your life. It's worse when the stranger is from your own family, so to say, and really ought *not* to be a stranger. Choose a girl from among one or another of the many other families of the world, so that if she turns out to be a stranger, as she is more than likely to do, at least it will be reasonable for her to be a stranger, and you won't ever feel quite so astonished, so disbelieving, or so eager for her to stop being a stranger. Look among the Norwegians."

"Why the Norwegians?"

"They're from the north and we're from the south. It ought to work out well for both of you, but especially for the children, who are of course what we are always really concerned about."

"Okay. I'll look around for a Norwegian girl."

"There is a colony of them around Kingsburg. I'll take you there in my carriage next year. Start taking a good look at them from a safe distance at an early age."

"Okay, but I really believed that you, of all people, would want every Bashmanian to marry an Armenian."

"I married an Armenian. Don't you, too."

"Okay."

"But even from among the Norwegians choose a girl who isn't so beautiful and so exciting that you instantly lose your wits, run a temperature, and go mad."

"I want to love the girl that I marry, don't I?"

"Of course you do, but that's precisely what I'm saying. Be sure it *is* you."

"How will I know?"

"From being able to think in her presence, from not being stupid in her presence, and from being able to talk with her about the things you are actually talking about. When you find that the things you are actually talking about are *not* the things you are talking about, that's when you know you're sick. Our whole family is stupid in this matter. We have always married the wrong women. We have always resisted learning. We don't learn anything until, as it is with me right now, it's too late. We like to believe we are a great family, but it's all a lie. Don't make the same stupid mistake I made, and all the rest of us made. Will you remember what I have told you?"

"Well, I'll try."

"Try very hard. It may save your life, your real life, not an imitation of your real life. And it may save the family, too."

He went out, and the years went by, just as I had always known they would, but in the end I didn't remember what he told me. I turned out to be as stupid as any other Bashmanian. I met a girl I had never expected to meet, not Norwegian, not Armenian, not any nationality at all, most likely. I fell in love, I ran a temperature, went mad, and we had four very good-looking kids, first two boys, and then two girls, all of them stupid, although in a way rather nice, too.

1975

The Last Word Was Love

A LONG TIME AGO when I was eleven my mother and my father had a prolonged quarrel.

The quarrel picked up the minute my father got home from work at Graff's, where he was a forty-seven-year-old assistant—to everybody. Graff's sold everything from food to ready-made clothing, animal traps, and farm implements. My father had taken the job only for the daily wage of three dollars, which he received in coin at the end of every twelve-hour day. He didn't mind the nature of the work, even though his profession was teaching, and he didn't care that it might end at any moment, without notice.

He'd already had the job six months, from late summer to early spring, when the quarrel began to get on my brother's nerves. I didn't even begin to notice the quarrel until Ralph pointed it out to me. I admired him so much that I joined him in finding fault with my mother and father.

First, though, I'd better describe the quarrel, if that's possible.

To begin with, there was my mother running the house, and there was my father working at Graff's. There was my brother, Ralph, at the top of his class at high school. There I was near the bottom of my class at junior high. And there was our nine-year-old sister, Rose, just enjoying life without any fuss.

All I can say about my mother is that she was a woman— to me a very beautiful one. She had a way of moving very quickly from a singing-and-laughing gladness to a silent-and-dark discontent that bothered my father. I remember hearing him say to her again and again, "Ann, what *is* it?"

Alas, the question was always useless, making my mother cry and my father leave the house.

During the long quarrel my father seemed hopelessly perplexed and outwitted by something unexpected and unwelcome, which he was determined nevertheless to control and banish.

My brother, Ralph, graduated from high school and took a summertime job in a vineyard. He rode eleven miles to the vineyard on his bicycle every morning soon after daybreak and back again a little before dark every evening. His wages were twenty-five cents an hour, and he put in at least ten hours a day. Early in September he had saved a little more than a hundred dollars.

Early one morning he woke me up.

"I want to say good-bye now," he said. "I'm going to San Francisco."

"What for?"

"I can't stay here any more."

Except for the tears in his eyes, I believe I would have said, "Well, good luck, Ralph," but the tears made that impossible. He was as big as my father. The suit he was wearing was my father's, which my mother had altered for him. What were the tears for? Would I have them in my own eyes in a moment, too, after all the years of imitating him to never have

them, and having succeeded except for the two or three times
I had let them go when I had been alone, and nobody knew?
And if the tears came into my eyes, too, what would they be
for? Everything I knew I'd learned from my brother, not from
school, and everything he knew he'd learned from my father.
So now what did we know? What did my father know? What
did my brother? What did I?

I got out of bed and jumped into my clothes and went
outside to the backyard. Under the old sycamore tree was the
almost completed raft my brother and I had been making in
our spare time, to launch one day soon on Kings River.

"I'll finish it alone," I thought. "I'll float down Kings
River alone."

My brother came out of the house quietly, holding an
old straw suitcase.

"I'll finish the raft," I said. I believed my brother would
say something in the same casual tone of voice, and then turn
and walk away, and that would be that.

Instead, though, he set the suitcase down and came to
the raft. He stepped onto it and sat down, as if we'd just
launched the raft and were sailing down Kings River. He put
his hand over the side, as if into the cold water of Kings River,
and he looked around, as if the raft were passing between vine-
yards and orchards. After a moment he got up, stepped out of
the raft, and picked up the suitcase. There were no tears in his
eyes now, but he just couldn't say goodbye. For a moment I
thought he was going to give up the idea of leaving home and
go back to bed.

Instead, he said, "I'll never go into that house again."
"Do you hate them? Is that why?"

"No," he said, but now he began to cry, as if he were eight or nine years old, not almost seventeen.

I picked up the raft, tipped it over, and jumped on it until some of the boards we had so carefully nailed together broke. Then I began to run. I didn't turn around to look at him again.

I ran and walked all the way to where we had planned to launch the raft, about six miles. I sat on the riverbank and tried to think.

It didn't do any good, though. I just didn't understand, that's all.

When I got home it was after eleven in the morning, I was very hungry, and I wanted to sit down and eat. My father was at his job at Graff's. My sister was out of the house, and my mother didn't seem to want to look at me. She put food on the table—more than usual, so I was pretty sure she knew something, or at any rate suspected.

At last she said, "Who smashed the raft?"

"I did."

"Why?"

"I got mad at my brother."

"Why?"

"I just got mad."

"Eat your food."

She went into the living room, and I ate my food. When I went into the living room she was working at the sewing machine with another of my father's suits.

"This one's for you," she said.

"When can I wear it?"

"Next Sunday. It's one of your father's oldest, when he was slimmer. It'll be a good fit. Do you like it?"

"Yes."

She put the work aside and tried to smile, and then *did*, a little.

"She doesn't know what's happened," I thought. And then I thought, "Maybe she *does*, and this is the way she is."

"Your brother's bike is in the garage," she said. "Where's *he?*"

"On his way to San Francisco."

"Where have you been?"

"I took a walk."

"A *long* walk?"

"Yes."

"Why?"

"I wanted to be alone."

My mother waited a moment and then she said, "Why is your brother on his way to San Francisco?"

"Because—" But I just couldn't tell her.

"It's all right," she said. "Tell me."

"Because you and Pop fight so much."

"*Fight?*"

"Yes."

"*Do we?*" my mother said.

"I don't know. Are you going to make him come home? Is Pop going to go and get him?"

"No."

"Does he *know?*"

"Yes. He told me."

"When?"

"Right after you ran off, and your brother began to walk to the depot. Your father saw the whole thing."

"Didn't he want to stop him?"

"No. Now, go out and repair the raft."

I worked hard every day and finished the raft in two weeks. One evening my father helped me get it onto a truck he'd hired. We drove to Kings River, launched it, and sailed down the river about twelve miles. My father brought a letter out of his pocket and read it out loud. It was addressed to Dear Mother and Father. All it said was that Ralph had found a job that he liked, and was going to go to college when the fall semester began, and was well and happy. The last word of the letter was love.

My father handed me the letter and I read the word for myself.

That Christmas my father sent me to San Francisco to spend a few days with my brother. It was a great adventure for me, because my brother was so different now—almost like my father, except that he lived in a furnished room, not in a house full of people. He wanted to know about the raft, so I told him I'd sailed it and had put it away for the winter.

"You come down next summer and we'll sail it together, the way we'd planned," I said.

"No," he said. "We've *already* sailed it together. It's all yours now."

My own son is sixteen years old now, and has made me aware lately that his mother and I have been quarreling for some time. Nothing new, of course—the same general quarrel—but neither his mother nor I had ever before noticed that it annoyed him. Later on this year, or perhaps next year, I know he's going to have a talk with *his* younger brother, and then take off. I want to be ready when that happens, so I can keep his mother from trying to stop him. He's a good boy, and I don't mind at all that he thinks I've made a mess of my life, which is one thing he is *not* going to do.

Of course he isn't.

1974

The Duel

Trash bashmanian was very good at public speaking, although he was better at pitching horseshoes and dueling. He was also quite good at taking a dare, and would jump off a high branch of a tree as if it were nothing. The dueling was real swordsmanship, which was taught him by a Frenchman who lived on L Street, not from our house in Fresno, and who somehow persuaded somebody to let him give free lessons to kids at the nearby California Playground every afternoon from four to five and all day Saturday.

The announcement appeared one day on the bulletin board at the playground, and Trash and several of his Portuguese pals and Armenian cousins, seeing the word "free" in the notice, were there the following afternoon for the first lesson. "I've been dueling all my life," Trash said to the Frenchman, referring to the stick duels he had enjoyed with anybody at school who had been willing to take him on. But the Frenchman produced a pair of ancient foils, authentic dueling devices surely brought over from his lost life in Paris, and was able to demonstrate that dueling wasn't quite just a matter of thrashing about with broomsticks. It was a courteous if deadly sport, very near the outskirts of art. Trash soon became his star pupil, and Trash's favorite expression became "On guard!"

Trash, older than me by two or three years, was a real
friend as well as a first cousin, and he was excessively cheerful
for a Bashmanian. For instance, he never thought of his first
name as an insult or even a friendly disparagement, no matter
who said it. "Trash" was actually only an ignorant American
rendering of his perfectly proper Armenian name, Artarash.
The first teacher he had had at Emerson School hadn't been
able to pronounce the name, so Artarash became Trash, and
by the time Trash was eight or nine he had almost forgotten
Artarash. He was twelve going on thirteen when he took up
dueling, and was already a champion horseshoe thrower. He
was certainly always able to throw a ringer at will, especially
for a penny bet. As for taking a dare, he stood alone in our
whole world, until one day, after highdiving into the very shal-
low water of Thompson Ditch, near Malaga, and almost breaking both arms, he suddenly realized that for years he had been
risking his life for no profit whatever. A few days later, he re-
marked, as if he had gone into another line of business, "I
don't take dares anymore," and that was the end of the matter.

At this time, back in 1919, public speaking was a highly
regarded talent in Fresno, and Trash was the best talker in
town. He did his speaking at schools, churches, picnics, and
Fourth of July celebrations. In a pinch, he could be counted
on to use up anywhere from five to twenty-five minutes, without preparation. He spoke in a voice that was not his regular
voice. It had a higher pitch, and as it went along it acquired a
rather musical quality, almost as if he were humming the speech
or even singing it, and now and then during his speeches he
actually broke into songs, to illustrate something or other that
he thought needed illustrating.

Trash could talk on any subject, most likely because he

knew that nobody was really listening in any case. During a talk at the Courthouse Park, for instance, he suddenly said, "That is why we have the Fourth of July," even though the preceding part of the speech had been about the Conestoga wagon. What's more, he heard instant applause. In the tradition of popular oratory, Trash started a talk at random, moved confidently ahead in no particular direction, and, although he spoke very clearly, said nothing.

After Masoor Franswah (as his students were instructed to call him) had taught him dueling, Trash frequently during a speech made a classical charge followed by a withdrawal movement, without explanation. He also kicked his right leg backward three or four times, again without explanation. Once when he did this, during a speech on civic pride, at the Parlor Lecture Club, his audience of women, eager to be cultured, burst into joyous giggles, accompanied by applause, which Trash believed was for what he had just said.

"What was that backward kicking for?" I asked him on our way home.

"I had a cramp. I had to kick it out," Trash said.

"What about the dueling?"

"What dueling?"

"Three or four times during your talk, you did some dueling."

"How did it go over?" he asked.

"All right, I guess," I said. "But what was it for?"

"Just a little decoration."

"But you've done the backward kicking and the dueling in the last three public speeches you've made."

"I get a cramp, I kick backwards. I need a decoration, I make a decoration," Trash said.

"I thought you were practicing, so you could duel some-body," I said. "I mean the way they used to duel in the old days—for keeps. At dawn, down by the river, for honor."

"Yes, that is what I want to do," Trash said.

"With real swords?"

"Yes, with real swords."

"For keeps?"

"I'll decide that at the time of the duel," Trash said. "I'll draw blood, but I may not kill."

"When's it going to be?"

"According to Masoor Franswah, two things are neces-sary," Trash said. "I've got to be insulted. Then I hit him on both sides of the face with a glove, and he's got to accept the challenge."

"Have you got a glove?"

"I've got the glove I wear when I play left field."

"You hit him across the face with *that* and he'll accept the challenge, all right," I said.

"I hope so," Trash said.

"Who's it going to be?" I asked.

"Who's been insulting me?"

"How about Miss Clifford?" I said. This was his teacher at Emerson School.

"Miss Clifford insults everybody in the sixth grade," Trash said. "Besides, it's got to be a man."

"A boy, don't you mean?"

"A boy's insults don't count," Trash said. "You hit him one in the nose and that's the end of it. If I'm going to swipe— if I'm going to borrow Masoor Franswah's swords and draw blood and maybe kill, it's got to be a man. So who's been pass-ing remarks behind my back? In the male adult community?"

"Nobody, Trash," I said. "Everybody likes you. You make these patriotic public speeches. You start them all just right and end them all just right. 'Mr. Chairman, Mrs. Chairman, Mrs. Chairman's mother, Dr. Rowell, Mr. Setrakinn, members of the Board of Education, ladies and gentlemen, boys and girls,' and all that other stuff at the beginning. And then at the end, how about the prayer that you say, that makes tears come to the eyes of so many people? 'Almighty God, let me try to be like Lincoln, not like Booth.' Who's Booth, Trash?"

"The dirty little sneak that shot Mr. Lincoln, that's who," Trash said. "Listen, has anybody been passing remarks behind your back? You're my kid cousin, you know."

"I don't think so, excepting members of the family," I said, "but it's always in front of my back."

"Members of the family don't count, either," Trash said. "Think hard. Who do I hate?"

"You don't hate anybody, Trash. Unless it's that dirty little sneak, Booth."

"He's been dead for years," Trash said. "I *know* I hate somebody, but I just can't seem to remember who. Let me think. Isn't there somebody we all hate?"

"Each other once in a while, is all I can remember."

"That's different."

"How about Masoor Franswah?"

"He's my friend," Trash said. "That little Frenchman taught me everything I know about being civilized."

"Do you hate Italians, maybe?" I asked.

"No, of course not."

"How about Germans? Indians? Mexicans? Hindus? Japanese? Serbians? Chinese? Portuguese? Negroes? Spaniards?"

"No, I like them all."

"Then you better forget about drawing blood," I said.

"It isn't a matter of forgetting," Trash said. "It's a matter of honor."

"What *is* honor?" I said. "I mean, what is it?"

"Honor?"

"Yes, Trash."

"Well, honor is . . . *yourself.* Every Bashmanian in the world has got a lot of himself."

"I never heard of any of them dueling anybody," I said.

"I'm the first Bashmanian who knows how. Find out who I hate and let me know, will you?"

The next day, he came to my house, and I was ready for him. "Trash," I said, "I think I found out who you hate."

"Who?"

"Turks."

"You're right," he said. "I *knew* there was somebody I hate. Now we're getting somewhere." He picked up a stick and began to duel, and he looked very good. "Who's a Turk, in town?"

"We've got Assyrians, Syrians, Persians, and maybe a few Arabs," I said.

"There's got to be a Turk somewhere in town, too," Trash said.

"Well, there's Ahboudt," I said. "You know—the man I work for in the Free Market Saturdays. I'm there from six in the morning until three in the afternoon, for twenty-five cents and a paper sack full of whatever he's stuck with. How about *him?*"

"Ahboudt? *Sounds* Turkish," Trash said. "Ask him. Let me know."

The following Saturday, I asked Ahboudt, and he looked at me in a funny way, and then he said, "Shine the eggplants, please." At the end of the day, when he gave me the quarter, he said, "Are you asking the Turk question for the government, or for yourself?"

"For my self, Mr. Ahboudt."

"I am not a Turk," he said. "I am an Arab." And then, "Christian."

"Do you know a Turk?" I asked.

"Why?"

"My cousin Trash wants to duel him."

"Why does he want to do that?"

"Trash likes everybody except Turks," I said, "and you only duel people you don't like. Is there a Turk somewhere in town?"

"There was a Turk," Ahboudt said, "but he was an old man and he died."

I passed along this information to Trash, who said, "I've got to find me a Turk. Enough is enough. I've got an idea. Be ready at seven o'clock at your house, and I'll take you with me to the Civic Auditorium tonight."

"The wrassling matches?"

"No, they're having New Citizens' Night. Maybe one of them will be a Turk, God willing."

"Are you going to make a public speech?"

"I may be called on to address the new Americans," Trash said.

When he came by at a quarter to seven and we started

walking to the Civic Auditorium, I said, "Have you got your speech ready?"

"I think so."

"What's your topic this time?"

"If Mayor Toomey asks me to get up on the stage and talk for ten minutes, the way he usually does, I'm going to say something about the real meaning of America."

"What are you going to say?"

"In America we forget old hatreds," Trash said. "Now nobody is anybody else's enemy. We are all members of the same family. We are all Americans. When we arrived in America, we stopped being what we were for so long."

I recognized this as something I had already heard six or seven times in class at Emerson School.

"Well, I don't think the Bashmanians stopped being what *they* were," I said.

Trash brought his outfielder's glove from the back pocket of his pants and studied it, and then he studied me.

"What's the matter?" I said.

"You're the first man who has ever insulted me," he said. "Me, Trash Bashmanian, patriotic American. And you're my own kid cousin, my own *first* kid cousin. I've known you all your life. I don't know what to do."

"Well, don't hit me with that glove," I said, "because I don't know anything about dueling, and if I insulted you I didn't mean to, and I apologize."

"Thank God," Trash said. "Apology accepted. Don't ever do it again—you don't know what happened to me when you said what you said."

"What happened?"

"My blood boiled."

"I'm sorry," I said, "but I was really surprised when you said that in America nobody is anybody else's enemy, because for two weeks I've been looking all over town for a Turk for you to duel and maybe kill."

"So what?" Trash said. "When you find the Turk, let me know, that's all. I'll think of something."

At the Civic Auditorium, we took seats in the first row, and right from the beginning everything began to go a little wrong, which was all right with me. At ten minutes to eight, Mayor Toomey said, "Dr. Chester Rowell, who is to make the main talk of the evening has been unavoidably detained, and Miss Shakay Takmakjian, who is to render a violin solo, has not yet arrived, so our program is unfortunately off schedule. We have a few minutes of spare time, and therefore it gives me great pleasure to call on our young friend Trash Bashmanian to come up here and . . . say something."

Trash jumped out of his seat, ran to the steps, and was standing beside Mayor Toomey by the time the Mayor said, "Ladies and gentlemen, Trash Bashmanian."

Crossing himself quickly but almost casually, like a professional man of God, Trash launched into another of his famous public addresses.

"What is America?" he asked in his high-pitched, special voice, and that was all he needed to get the glory and the oratory rolling. Soon he was asking a lot of other unanswerable questions, and talking smoothly, and now and then suddenly dueling or kicking backward. After about twelve minutes, it seemed as if Trash was about to bring his talk to an end, but Mayor Toomey called out from the side of the stage, "A few minutes more, Trash," and Trash changed from a concluding tone to a tone of starting up again. He was just getting into the swing of this new start when Mayor Toomey called out, "Tie it up, Trash. Here he is." And so, simultaneously dueling and kicking backward, Trash paused, looked upward, and said, "Almighty God, let me try to be like Woodrow Wilson, not Henry Ford."

The audience rose to its feet and broke into applause— perhaps because the first citizen of the city, Dr. Chester Rowell, had just appeared on the stage. Trash bowed, but only once, and came down the steps and sat down.

On our way home, I said, "You sure told 'em, Trash."

"What did I say?"

"You said we are all brothers—all of us—just as Washington, Jefferson, Jackson, and Caruso taught us to be."

"Who?"

"That's what I was wondering."

"Did I put Caruso in there with those other guys?" he asked.

"Yes. What'd you do it for?"

"I don't know," Trash said, "but there must be a reason."

"And then you sang 'O Sole Mio,' " I said.

"I *knew* there was a reason," Trash said. "It was so I could sing the song he sings on that Victor Red Seal phonograph record at our house. How was my voice?"

"It was good," I said.

"Was my diction all right, singing the Italian words?"

"I guess so," I said. "It certainly sounded like Italian to me. You won't be wanting me to find a Turk any more then, will you?"

"Why not?"

"Because you told me in your speech not to."

"I *did?*" Trash said.

"Yes. Don't you remember when you were coming to the end of the talk the first time—before Mayor Toomey told you to keep going? Well, you were almost singing a lot of other things, kind of humming the words, and then all of a sudden you said, 'Look not in the world for the Turk, you will not find him there.' "

" 'Look not in the world for the Turk, you will not find him there'?" Trash repeated.

"That's right."

We walked along in silence for quite a while, and then Trash said, "Was it a good public speech, would you say?"

"Very good," I said.

"As good as my others?"

"Better," I said. "But no more of this Turk business then—is that right? No duel, no drawing of blood? 'Look not in the world for the Turk, you will not find him there.' That's what you said, Trash."

"What a fool I was," Trash said. "Now what am I going to do with all this dueling talent?"

What he did was have me take lessons from Masoor Franswah, so that now and then we could take turns being the Turk in the world, and in our own hearts, each of us winning and losing every time, whichever side we took.

1976

A Letter from William Saroyan to James Laughlin

SAROYAN

348 Carl Street.
San Francisco.
November 20,
1938.

— of the enemy

Dear Jim:

The day the New Directions books (second series)
arrived, I wrote you again; the day after,your letter
of November 11th came, for which many thanks. I have
waited these few days before writing again, hoping the
rejected manuscript would arrive, and I would write and
say it had---but it hasn't yet. But surely will soon.

About the New Directions War: well, the poor
bookstore keepers aren't the enemy, although in a
tragicly silly way they are allies: these poor people
are trying to get a living out of <u>selling</u> books, and
after a while the selling of the noblest thing in the
world becomes a horrible activity; you have only to
think of the women who sell it. The only kind of
books the booksellers will order is the kind they
think will find buyers quick and without trouble.
I used to get sore at the bookstore owners or managers
for ordering,six copies of my books; now I ask them if
they aren't afraid they'll get stuck; and sometimes I
say let me know if you get stuck; I'll buy the copies
you cant sell. If one of my books gets out of the red
I'm satisfied---because this means the publisher will
not be terribly afraid to publish another one. I don't *followed by*
know who the real enemy is, Jim, unless it's ourselves;
them our equals or superiors who read but don't write;
it's a cinch we don't stand a chance in the world with
the people; they're busy with other things; we have an
ally in youth, I believe, but as a rule youth reads, does
not buy,books. I thought Modern Age books would sell
like hotcakes in the universities, but I hear they didn't.
Because, reduced to its simplest meaning, a book is an hour
or two of reading, and because reading is a passive, not an
active or dynamic event of experience for the people,
we are, whether we like it or not, in competition with the
newspapers, which are everywhere all the time, the magazines,
and with the book that has been in every family sixty years
or so, which is sometimes The Bible, sometimes a leather-bound
volume of Bulwer-Lyton. (For instance.) There is little
interest in New directions in living, so it is natural that
there shall be still less in N.D. in writing---which is the

only

A Letter from William Saroyan to James Laughlin

prelude in some cases, the postlude in others, to N.D.
in living. To us, no doubt, there can be no decent living
without decent writing; we need and demand and make one,
on behalf of the other. We ourselves, however, *are* several
thousand light years from the truth, from a decent reality;
a reality with dimension, order, reason, spontaneity,
and dozens of other good things---and that's why I say
that we ourselves are our own enemies. Some of our
greatest writing has been great because it has been
evil---evil is that which disintegrates the Man, that's
all: good is that which integrates; the world disintegrated
man first; we reported what the world had done, and because
what it had *be* done was so vast and tragic our reporting
was, in one sense at least, great: James Joyce; poor Lawrence,
trying to become integrated personally and thereby
trying to save the whole race; many others along the way;
and now Henry (Miller). These men were or will be burned
by the enormity of the task and will die, or have died,
before they will have reached the light, and balanced the
labor: given it dimension; inhaled, and, exhaled; and
put the good over the evil, showing the fuller reality
of the two together, as they certainly are, from birth;
until the good is over the evil (but the evil is known
to be beneath) our writing is not truly great. Two
things, seemingly unrelated but actually closely related, *inevitably*
raise hell with the worker for *this* literature
and living: money and sex; both are irritants potentially
all the time, and needn't be. No one I know of is waging
a fiercer war with these two than Henry in Paris. As far
as I can tell from his writing, I mean. Having neither one
nor the other does one thing to the Man; and squandering
one or the other, or both, does another thing to him; both
usually evil, but sorrowfully. If the spendthrift hasn't
money, he wastes the life in himself, in desperation---and
for several dozen possible reasons, or out of that many
impulses. The truly great tribe of writers is yet to be
born. There isn't yet enough true pride in them---there
is a ferocious pride at times, now, but it's full of deep
wretchedness.

The paragraph's too long.

I feel pretty certain of this, though: that you
won't be knowing the real importance of New Directions
for fifteen or twenty years, even if you stop next year, or
the year after---or even if you keep going fifteen or twenty
years.

A Letter from William Saroyan to James Laughlin

3

I have a swell book of around 50,000 words ~~far~~
called A FINE HOW DO YOU DO, consisting of around 25
short pieces, which are very much the McCoy, but perhaps
something Harcourt would rather some ~~one~~ other house
published---the important thing, I believe, would be
to issue it at a time suitably in-between Harcourt
books, or in this case, in March or April, 1939---
the book can be shortened or lengthened, whichever
is preferred. I believe Hardourt would gladly give
New Directions permission to do the book, if you happened
to like it. ~~████████████~~ Let me know when you'll
have time to look the stuff over, *and I'll send it along.*

The $20. I shall send out of the first check,
which should come by the 26th---unless The Group
Theatre won't compromise on our contract---they've
more or less accepted My Heart's in the Highlands,
but the contract they offered me had a clause in it
that I couldn't take, even though I needed the advance
very badly---when the $300. advance does arrive, it
will last not more than three days: THE DEBTS. The
patient, vicious, beautiful, ever-present debts.

About the stories by me still unprinted: send
me two or three sets of proofs of each---and I'll
correct them and include them with the material in
A Fine How Do You Do. And for New Directions 1939,
I'll give you something very brand new and good.

As I said in Three Times Three, the new book *(The Trouble etc.)*
is of course only another chapter to The Book. I'm
one man and I'm writing one book. (As soon as you
let me know that you want to see A Fine Etc., I'll
write to Harcourt and ask; you can write too anytime
at all, if you like; the important thing will be to
be able to tell them approximately when the book will
appear.) With best regards:

Bill